SUMMER NIGHTS AND PILLOW FIGHTS

BETH RAIN

Copyright © 2021 by Beth Rain

Summer Nights and Pillow Fights (Little Bamton: Book 3)

First Publication: 30th April, 2021

All rights reserved.

No part of this book may be reproduced in any form or by any electronic or mechanical means, including information storage and retrieval systems. Except for use in any review, the reproduction or utilization of this work, in whole or in part, in any form by any electronic, mechanical or other means now known or hereafter invented, is forbidden without the written permission of the publisher.

Published by Beth Rain. The author may be contacted by email on bethrainauthor@gmail.com

CHAPTER 1

It was taking every ounce of Eve's determination not to let her quivering lip get the better of her. After eighteen years of practice, she was usually pretty good at hiding her emotions when she needed to - and she was damned if she was going to fall at this last hurdle.

'Are you ready lad?'

The gruff voice of her ex-husband made every muscle in her body tighten uncomfortably. His presence in her home felt so wrong after all these years. This was her sanctuary from the world - a home she'd worked hard to make as cosy and comfortable as possible for her and Davy. Rhys had moved out when Davy was just two years old. Sixteen years was a long time - but even now, she hated the feeling of him being in their space. Her space. In fact, she hated it more than ever today.

'Almost, dad,' yelled Davy from the sitting room, where he was busy shoving a few last bits and pieces into his already over-stuffed rucksack. 'Just want to check my room one last time - I think I left my phone charger up there.'

'I'll wait for you in the car. Hurry up.'

Eve winced as she listened to Davy thundering his way up the stairs - it was a habit she'd never quite managed to wean him off, no matter how hard she'd tried.

'Bye then, Eve,' said Rhys.

Eve whipped around to respond, only to catch a glimpse of the back of his head as he disappeared out through the door, back to the safety of his car.

Unbelievable. That was all he had to say for himself after swooping in and messing up the perfect summer she'd had planned with her boy?

It was going to be her last summer with Davy before he went to uni. She'd been looking forward to spending some down-time with him now that the stress of his A-Levels was over and they could both finally relax in the knowledge that his place at Cardiff uni was secure.

'Yeah. See ya,' Eve grunted as the front door swung closed behind him, and then for good measure, she stuck her tongue out too. It was amazing, but after all this time the man could still turn her from a sensible (ish) mother and (mostly) functioning adult into a cantankerous toddler.

Eve ran her hands through her hair and then gave herself a little shake. She needed to pull herself together - just for a little bit longer. She might not like the way Rhys had gone about luring Davy away for the summer, but there was no way she was going to let her boy catch even the faintest whiff of her disappointment. All she wanted was for him to be happy. That was all she'd *ever* wanted. There would be plenty of time for wobbly lips and tears when he'd gone.

Just moments later, Davy came hurtling back down the stairs with a bag slung carelessly over one shoulder - presumably holding the last bits he wanted to take away with him. No doubt his room would be a complete tip - the remnants of a long and fun-filled childhood (that he wouldn't be caught dead taking to uni with him) scattered across the floor in his hunt for holiday essentials.

'Bye mum - I'll call you when we get to dad's.'

Eve nodded. 'And you'll message me as soon as you can when you get to Greece?'

Davy nodded.

Eve could tell he was doing his best not to roll his eyes at her, and she was grateful. She couldn't help fussing - he'd always be her little boy. She had to keep reminding herself that he was, in fact, a grown adult. It should be a lot easier, considering he was a whole foot taller than her at six foot two inches. But every time she looked at his face, complete with a rebellious hint of bum-fluff-beard now that he'd left school, all she could see was the mischievous, kind-hearted little boy he'd always been.

Eve could feel the tears threatening to spill again, so she quickly opened her arms for a hug and Davy didn't hesitate to gather her to him, wrapping his ridiculously long arms around her.

When had her little boy with his Thomas the Tank obsession turned into this thoughtful, handsome man-child? Eve buried her face in his teeshirt, doing her best to pull herself together.

'You'll be okay, won't you mum?' he asked into her hair.

Eve tightened her arms around him for a second longer, before holding him out in front of her and smiling up at him.

'Of course. I'll be fine. I want you to have the best summer, okay?'

Davy nodded, a frown on his handsome face.

'Really, Davy. You make the most of this trip. It's brilliant that you'll get to spend this time with your dad and Chell and your little brothers, okay?'

He nodded again. 'I love you, mum.'

Eve swallowed hard. 'I love you too, Davy-boy. So much. And I can't wait to hear about everything you get up to, okay?'

She pulled him back into her chest and hugged him hard one last time.

HONK!

The blare of the car horn outside sent a shockwave

through her and it was as much as she could do to contain a growl. Why was it that, every time she was forced to see him, Rhys seemed determined to underline reasons she'd been better off without him? Beeping the bloody horn? Really?! He'd have half the village over to check what was happening if he carried on like that.

'I'd better go, mum.'

Eve nodded. 'Have an amazing time.' She reached out and ruffled his hair just like she had thousands of times before - but this time Davy managed to grin at her instead of uttering the teenaged grumble it usually elicited.

'Bye love,' she said, trying her best to swallow the sob that was busy rising up in her throat.

'Mum - are you sure you're going to be okay?' he asked again, one hand on the front door handle - clearly desperate to head off on his adventure.

Eve forced herself to smile at him. 'Are you kidding me? Of course I am. Parties every night without you to cramp my style.'

Davy grinned back at her even as he raised his eyebrows in complete disbelief. 'Yeah right. I won't recognise you when I come back, will I?'

Eve blinked hard - keeping this smile in place was turning out to be quite painful.

'Nope,' she said, not trusting herself to answer in any more detail just in case she betrayed the fact that her heart felt like it was breaking.

'Well . . . just don't trash the house, okay?' he said, in a mock-stern tone.

Eve saluted, and then moved to stand in the doorway as Davy jogged towards the waiting car.

Twenty minutes of full-blown ugly-crying face-down on the kitchen table later, Eve decided that enough was enough. She grabbed a handful of kitchen-roll and mopped her sopping face, taking deep, steadying breaths.

'Enough!' she said out loud with a shaky laugh. After all, she'd known this day was coming. It was inevitable that Davy was going to leave home and head off on adventures of his own. It was time for him to start his own life, and she wouldn't deny him that for anything. But . . . well, she had expected him to be around for a few more weeks. Bloody Rhys.

Eve sighed and stood up. It was time to go and rescue any washing-up and stray bits of dirty washing from Davy's room before they had the chance to create a new civilisation in there.

The house seemed eerily silent now that she was here on her own. Of course, she'd been here alone plenty of times before - like when Davy had been staying over with his mates or out at one of the many hockey practices he was addicted to - but this was different. Maybe it was because she knew that he wouldn't be back. Or at least, not in the same way. Ah crap, here came the tears again.

Eve swallowed hard and made her way along the long upstairs hallway. This house had always been on the extravagant side for the two of them. She'd bought it with Rhys before they were married - when they'd been ecstatically planning a huge family together. She'd coughed up a vast chunk of her own money for the whopping deposit. At the time, it had been the only way to make sure that the mortgage would be manageable - and she was certain that her great-aunt, who'd left her the money, would have approved.

That's why, when everything had gone wrong and they'd separated, Eve had fought tooth-and-nail to keep the house. It was a decision she'd never regretted, even if it meant she'd probably still be paying the mortgage by the time she was drawing her pension. That's if she decided to stay here, of course.

She couldn't imagine leaving this house - leaving Little Bamton. It was her home. But what did a single-woman on the wrong side of forty need with a six-bedroom farmhouse, complete with its own acre of garden?

Eve let out an impatient huff. Now was not the time to start working through that particular dilemma.

Pushing her way into Davy's bedroom, she came to an abrupt stop, her heart squeezing painfully. Davy had taken enough possessions to see him through the summer, and over underneath the window was a stack of packed boxes, ready and waiting to accompany him to Cardiff in the autumn.

Even so, the room was still very much full of Davy - from the glow-in-the-dark stars on the ceiling that she'd stuck there for him when he was five years old, to the blackboard wall she'd created for him as a surprise for his fifteenth birthday. It was still covered with detailed designs for an eco-house he'd worked on for his college applications to study architecture.

It didn't matter that she'd raised their son pretty much single-handedly - with Rhys making the occasional holiday appearance - Davy was the perfect blend of the two of them. He'd inherited her artistic, creative side and Rhys's mathematical, detail-oriented side. Thank heavens he didn't get his dad's temper in the mix too.

Eve quickly moved into the room, grabbed a pint glass that was still half-full of Ribena, tossed an empty Pringles tube into the bin and generally shook her head at the "tidy" bedroom that needed a good tidy up - especially when it came to the amount of laundry that was currently strewn across the floor.

As she reached out to pull the navy and white checked duvet back into place on the bed, she spotted an envelope sitting on one of the dented pillows. There was a single word on the front. Mum.

Eve put everything down and sank onto the bed, taking the envelope in her hands. She flipped it over and let out a surprised laugh. On the back flap, written in Davy's close, tidy hand, were the words *"I knew you'd be in to tidy up as soon as I left!"*

With a trembling finger, Eve slit open the envelope, being careful not to tear the message on the back. She drew out a sheet of lined paper that looked like it had been torn from an exercise book and quickly unfolded it.

By the time she got to the end, she was a howling mess again. In his careful hand, Davy had poured out his love for her and the amazing years they had spent together. He'd thanked her for everything she'd done for him - everything he was sure she must have given up for him. But it was the last few lines that really set her off.

"It's time for you to have some adventures now too, mum! I can't wait to hear what you get up to (well . . . most of it!) Find someone who loves you like you deserve to be loved - and then make a life as beautiful as your paintings. Just don't give my room away - because I'm going to be visiting loads :) I love you.
Thank you for being my mum. Davy x"

CHAPTER 2

She was in a heap on the sofa when the doorbell rang. Eve quickly plonked down her now-cold cup of tea and then dragged the edge of the knitted patchwork blanket up to her face to mop her eyes.

She must look a mess. She'd been giving in to the waves of tears on and off for the past couple of hours, and she'd moved on to wiping her eyes with the blanket when the box of Kleenex had bitten the dust about half an hour ago - because she simply couldn't muster the energy to go to the pantry and get a fresh one

And now there was someone at the door. The temptation to ignore the ringing was huge, but this was Little Bamton - which meant ignoring the door just wasn't an option. Not unless you wanted the whole village to descend on you to check you were okay.

The villagers looked after their own. This was something she'd been so grateful for over the years, and something that had made raising Davy single-handedly a whole lot easier - because it hadn't been single-handed at all - Little Bamton was basically Davy's third parent. That being said, right now it felt more like a royal pain in the bum than a blessing.

'I'm coming, I'm coming!' she muttered as the bell trilled again, forcing her up off the sofa.

Eve quickly brushed down her jeans and scruffy old jumper, doing her best to smooth back her hair. She could swear this last few weeks dealing with Rhys and his plans for Davy's summer had added more grey streaks into the black than ever.

She headed towards the front door just as the bell trilled for the third time and, catching sight of herself in the hall mirror, she paused. Her eyes were pink and swollen - it couldn't be more obvious that she'd cried the afternoon away - and it wasn't like she could try to palm it off as a bout of hay fever - not a single person in the village would believe that.

'Eve - answer the door woman!' yelled a voice from outside. That had to be Lucy.

'Yeah Eve! I need a pee . . . so unless you want a puddle!'

Eve snorted. You could always count on Amber to lower the tone - even before you'd set eyes on her.

She hurried to open the door to her friends. They'd known her long enough that there was no way they'd

SUMMER NIGHTS AND PILLOW FIGHTS

go anywhere without checking she was alright. They knew all the ins and outs of the whole story with Rhys and Davy anyway - there had been several book-club meetings over the past few weeks that had been more about getting her through this than discussing the poor, abandoned novel of the week. Lucy and Amber were probably here to try to cheer her up. Well, if anyone could it was these two.

Okay, these five! Eve quickly amended as she opened the door only to come face to face with all five members of the book club. Amber, Lucy, Sue, Caro and Emmy were all standing there, arms laden with various bundles.

'Thank f . . . udge for that!' squeaked Amber. 'Do you mind?'

Eve let out a noise that was half-chuckle, half sob and stood aside to let her friend rush past her and straight to the under-stairs cupboard that she'd turned into a loo years ago.

'How're you doing, lovely?' asked Lucy, stepping forward to give her a one-armed hug while balancing a massive cake-box with her other hand.

'M'ok,' mumbled Eve, doing her best to keep it together.

'Course you're not,' said Sue, patting her shoulder as soon as Lucy let go of her. 'But you will be!' She waggled a couple of bottles of homemade wine at Eve, who winced as the memory of her last encounter with Sue's home-brew surfaced. The stuff was delicious but deceptively potent. She seemed to remember there had been quite a lot of singing involved last time.

'Hi Eve,' said Emmy, thrusting a massive bouquet of roses and feathery greenery into her arms.

'Hey Emmy! These are gorgeous, thank you! Old roses are-'

'Your favourites,' Emmy finished for her with a smile.

Eve just nodded and buried her nose in the flowers, letting the heady scent overwhelm her senses for a second as Emmy stepped past her into the house.

She finally looked up only to find Caro watching her intently.

'Caro! Sorry, I thought you'd gone in.'

Caro shook her head. 'Have you had enough of hugs or do I get one?'

'You can never have too many hugs,' said Eve, stepping forward and wrapping an arm around her friend.

'So - I haven't brought a pressie this evening, but-'

'No one needed to do that! I'm fine,' said Eve, easing back from the hug and linking arms with Caro as they stepped into the house.

'Of course you are. But what I was going to say is - when you're ready, come to the shop. I'm gifting you a little bit of a makeover to celebrate your newly acquired young, free single-hood.'

'Not sure about *young!*' replied Eve as she closed the door firmly behind the two of them. 'And I've been single forever...'

'Well - maybe *footloose, fabulous and fancy-free* works better for you?'

'I'll take that!' said Eve with a wan smile. She didn't feel any of those things right now, but it would definitely be nice.

'Right then, let's get this party started!' said Caro, pulling ahead of her to lead the way into the sitting room.

Eve paused a moment in the hall. What would she do without this bunch of nutters? Caro might only have moved to the village at Christmas - and Emmy even more recently than that - but along with the other three, they'd quickly become the voices of sanity in her life. They were a strange kind of constant as everything else started to shift around her.

Eve took a deep breath and let the scent of roses lift her spirits. The tension in her shoulders started to ease a little. Sure, Davy was off on his adventures, but maybe he was right and it was time to have some of her own too. The thing was, *how* exactly did you go about having an adventure in a village you'd lived in for twenty years?

A gale of laughter poured out of the sitting room, and she shook her head. If anyone could help her figure out *that* little conundrum, it was this wonderful bunch of women.

'You okay?'

Amber's voice behind her made her whizz around.

'Fine!' she said on autopilot.

Amber raised her eyebrows, looking her dead in the eye.

'Actually, thanks to you guys, I really am,' said Eve.

'In that case,' said Amber, winding an arm around her shoulders and marching her into the sitting room, 'let's get one of Sue's bottles on the go!'

'Alright - you have wine, you have flowers, you have cake-' said Emmy with a smile as Eve curled her feet up underneath her and settled into her favourite corner of the sofa.

'Prepare for a grilling!' laughed Lucy.

Eve smiled around at her friends and took a cautious sip of pea-pod wine. Supposedly it was a 2016 vintage. It was delicious, but she knew that it was also fairly likely to be deadly, so she'd be pacing herself. The last thing she needed was to wake up tomorrow with the hangover from hell.

'The question is - how are you *really* feeling about all this now that it's actually happened?' said Sue gently.

Eve cocked her head while she thought about this for a second. She was definitely feeling better now that she was surrounded by her friends, but she still had a heavy weight in her chest. It felt a lot like grief - which was stupid, wasn't it? Not to mention selfish. It was the most natural thing in the world for Davy to grow up and spread his wings. Surely she should be happy for him?!

'I feel like I've been robbed,' she said, surprising herself as the thought exited her mouth before she'd even processed it. 'I thought I had all summer to spend with Davy - you know, do our favourite things one last time before he officially moved out. Then along comes Rhys with his stupid, flashy gesture - as usual - and Davy's just gone.'

She stopped talking abruptly.

'Stupid, I know,' she muttered as an afterthought.

'Hell no!' cried Caro.

Lucy was shaking her head too, and the others were looking devastated.

'Caro's right,' said Sue. 'That's not even remotely stupid. You've not had much chance to process the fact that Davy was going to leave early. Not to mention that everything you've known for so long is shifting.'

'Erm, I think we're trying to make her feel better, not worse,' said Lucy in a stage-whisper.

Eve couldn't help but let out a laugh. 'Sue's right, though. That's how it feels. I'm out of control.'

'But Davy will be back just before he goes to uni, won't he?' said Emmy.

Eve nodded. 'For about a week.'

'And he's bound to visit loads,' said Amber.

Eve nodded again. 'Yeah, he will. And I know it's not like I'm losing him, but . . . well, he won't be living with me anymore.'

'Don't you count on that,' laughed Amber. 'My parents keep thinking they've finally got my brother to move out, but he just keeps coming back like a bad penny!'

Eve smiled, doing her best to squash down the irrational jealousy she now held for Amber's parents.

'It's really selfish - I just wish I'd had a bit more time with him.' She paused and took a large gulp of wine to give herself a moment to regain control.

'Well - I hate to say it, but the best thing you can do right now is to make some exciting new plans of your own,' said Lucy. 'You know, to reduce the likelihood of-'

'Moping?' Eve finished for her.

Lucy nodded, giving her a rueful smile.

'Yeah, you're probably right. And I guess the first thing I need to decide is whether I'm going to stay here or not.'

Eve's pronouncement almost caused a riot as all five of her friends started to argue with her at once. She gave up trying to get a word in edgeways as she listened to the babble of indignation at the mere suggestion that she might decide to move out of this house and away from Little Bamton. In fact, their unanimous horror at the idea was making her feel warm and loved . . . in a very weird kind of way.

'The question is,' said Sue, finally raising her voice of reason above the others, 'what do *you* want, Eve? To stay here in the village, or try somewhere new.'

Eve stared at her a moment and the others actually fell silent in order to hear her response.

'Erm . . . well . . . this is a huge house for one person.'

She looked around at them, waiting for them to agree, but to their credit, they all suddenly had their poker faces in place.

'I mean - it's home. Little Bamton's home. If I could find somewhere a bit smaller here maybe I'd really consider it, but you know what it's like?'

'Hen's teeth!' agreed Emmy, having recently been through that particular conundrum herself when there had been the chance that she'd have to move out of Dragonfly Cottage.

'Right,' said Eve with a shrug. 'So if I move, it'll have to be out of the village.'

'So that's a definite no-no,' said Caro, crossing her arms.

'Weeeelll . . .' said Eve. Her heart agreed with her friend, but . . . her head? The idea of rattling around this place - feeling lonely and missing Davy but not actually moving on with her own life - wasn't something she relished the thought of.

'Oh, come *on* Eve!! Don't break up the gang now!' said Amber.

'Okay, you're right - I don't want to. If I'm being honest, I really don't want to leave the village - or this house.'

'Can I ask a personal question?' said Sue quietly.

'Of course.'

'Is it a financial thing?'

Eve thought about this for a second, then shook her head. 'No. I've managed this place for a long time without any help. I've got it set up so that I can carry on doing that - it's tight but manageable. But . . . it *is* quite extravagant for one person to live in a place like this. I mean - one person, six bedrooms?!'

Eve was trying to make light of it with her friends, but in reality, she wanted to swap out the word "extravagant" for the word "lonely".

'It's not that different from just you and Davy living here, surely?' said Emmy, not quite catching on.

'Completely different,' sighed Eve. 'There's been a gaggle of kids in and out of this house for years. Now, with him gone, it's going to be so-'

'Lonely?' said Amber.

'I was going to say quiet - but yeah. It's going to be lonely.'

'Then we need to find an answer to that,' said Caro determinedly.

'You could get a lodger?' said Amber, prizing the top off the giant Tupperware tub Lucy had brought with her and helping herself to a chocolate cupcake.

Eve pulled a face. 'What if I ended up hating them? Or they hated me? That's a lot of commitment!'

'True! And don't hog the cakes,' laughed Caro, grabbing the box from Amber, taking one and passing it around.

'Well - how about dating?' said Emmy through a mouthful of thick, chocolate icing. 'We could set you up with some apps - you could meet some new people . . .'

'I can sense the *hell no* from all the way over here,' said Sue, smirking at the look of horror that was suddenly plastered on Eve's face.

'My life has just changed enough as it is, thanks very much,' she spluttered. 'Again - too much commitment!'

'Okay,' said Lucy, 'so let's just recap here a sec - you don't want the house to feel lonely or empty, but you don't want a lodger or any new long-term commitment, and you definitely aren't ready to start dating yet?'

'Sounds about right,' said Eve with a chuckle. 'Don't ask for much, do I?'

'Ask for the world!' said Caro. 'It's a great time to go after what you really want.'

'So Eve - what is it you want?' said Amber, wiggling her eyebrows.

Eve took a fortifying sip of her wine, trying to ignore the fact that all her friends were now gazing at her with rapt attention.

'Okay - one thing I'd love to do is a bit more teaching. Sharing my love of art with other people is something I really miss.'

'Have you done it before?' asked Emmy curiously.

Eve nodded. 'I used to be a guest lecturer down at

Plymouth uni, and sometimes I'd go down to Falmouth too.'

'Why'd you stop?' said Caro.

'Because most of the students on those courses turned out to be pretentious little sh... poops,' she said. 'Honestly - they were more into the idea of taking a bunch of broken glass, piling it under a streetlight and calling that "art" rather than learning any actual skill. They thought the craft side of things was so far beneath them - it was really frustrating!'

'Amen to that!' said Amber 'I've met a few of those types on my weaving courses!'

'So, if not the university gigs . . .?' said Sue curiously.

'Well, I've always fancied running private workshops. A week or two spent with a small group of people who are actually enthusiastic.'

'And that way, if you do get any stinkers, you can be shot of them pretty quickly,' said Amber.

'Exactly!' nodded Eve. 'But I've always struggled with where I could base them. Renting somewhere in Exeter or Plymouth would be way too pricey to start with - and anyway - I want to be here, in the village - near enough to do some of the teaching in the studio.'

'Then the answer's obvious,' laughed Caro.

'Erm . . . it is?' said Eve, staring at her.

Caro nodded. 'Turn this place into a B&B for your students and make the courses residential and based here in Little Bamton!'

'I couldn't . . . could I?' said Eve, staring wide-eyed back at Caro. But there was something in this. She knew there was because a tingle travelled down the length of her spine, making her shiver.

'You could,' said Sue, looking excited.

'You definitely could,' agreed Lucy, her eyes sparkling.

'Wow. Can you imagine? Davy left me a letter telling me to have some adventures of my own,' she said with a soft smile.

'Well,' laughed Amber, 'I'd say this would definitely count!'

CHAPTER 3

'Now then, are you sure?' asked Emmy, her finger hovering over her computer mouse.

It had been a week since Davy had left. A week since that memorable evening when her friends had tipped her world even further on its axis when they'd waltzed in to make sure that she was doing okay, fuelled her up with pea-pod wine and then casually suggested life-altering plans to her.

Was she sure?

It had been years since she'd worked this hard on a project. She'd put in hours of planning and preparation. Come to that, so had everyone else!

Sue and Lucy had helped her get the house ready, shifting years worth of random, accumulated crap out of the four guest bedrooms and cramming it (just for now, she promised herself) into Davy's recently vacated space. Then, between them, they'd given the bedrooms a thorough clean, a fresh coat of paint, and then Eve and Caro had spent a most enjoyable afternoon ordering new bedding and other pretty bits and bobs online.

Emmy had helped her to create a simple website for the workshops. They'd included some wonderfully artsy shots to show off the house and village too. Emmy had even managed to talk her into setting up an Instagram account and a Facebook page.

Everything was ready to go live - complete with her mobile phone number and email for bookings - all she had to do was press the button and this mad scheme would become her new reality.

'Definitely. I'm sure. Let's do it.'

'Click here then,' said Emmy, relinquishing the mouse and pointing at the screen in front of her instead.

She knew it was silly, but Eve had butterflies. But it wasn't as though anything was going to happen immediately, was it? She'd decided on two sets of workshop dates to start with, each one running for a week - and culminating a short public exhibition of her students' work in her studio.

Hopefully, this would be enough for her to test the waters. She could always add more dates or, alternatively, she could take the whole thing down if she decided she hated it. She wouldn't really have lost anything by giving it a try, other than the money she'd spent on the house - and those bedrooms looked much better for a sprucing up anyway!

She reached forward and clicked the mouse. A tingle ran down her spine, just as it had when they'd first talked about the idea. Was this fate - or was she just sitting in a draft?

'Woop!' squealed Emmy. 'Right, now let's post that link all over social media!'

Eve grinned at her friend and whipped out her mobile ready to christen her brand new Insta account with the graphic they'd prepared earlier.

'There. It's official. I'm actually doing this!' said Eve, admiring her first post.

'Yay! This is so exciting!'

Eve sat back from the desk and stared out at the beautiful walled garden of Dragonfly cottage, which was a riot of summer colour. Her throat seemed to tighten up for a moment as another wave of nerves hit her. She'd just bitten off quite a chunk of work. She'd been so focused on this new workshop idea along with the residential side of things that she hadn't really given much thought to how she was going to juggle it with keeping her studio in the craft centre going.

'You alright?' asked Emmy, grabbing their empty tea mugs and getting to her feet.

Eve nodded as she followed her friend through to

the kitchen where Eve's adopted tom-cat Charlie leapt up from his sunny spot to greet them.

'I'm fine, really,' she said, tickling Charlie's ears. 'Just wondering how on earth I'm going to make this all work.'

Emmy placed the cups down on the draining board and turned to her. 'I know that feeling!' she said. 'When I started Grandad Jim's - it all started out really simply - but then everything snowballed!'

Eve nodded. Emmy hadn't really been in the village all that long, but she couldn't imagine life here without her now - nor her blooming business. Eve enjoyed Emmy's flowers as much as everyone else in the village, and she was excited to see the flower farm go absolutely nuts - even though it was only in its first year.

'How did you deal with it all to start with?' she asked. 'You always seem so on top of everything!'

'Take it one job and one day at a time. It's good to have big plans, but really it's all just a list of tiny jobs strung together.'

'But you make it look so easy!' laughed Eve, Emmy's words comforting her in spite of herself.

'Well, I had a great bunch of new friends right behind me.'

Eve smiled at her, grabbing her hand and squeezing it.

'So do you,' added Emmy, 'and don't you forget it. Now - all you have to do is wait for the phone to ring!'

'Easy as that!' said Eve, waggling her mobile, and

then promptly dropping it onto the kitchen table as it started to vibrate in her hand.

She stared at Emmy who stared back at her, wide-eyed.

'It can't be . . . can it?' said Eve.

'I don't know,' whispered Emmy. 'Answer it and find out!'

Eve grabbed her phone, flipped open the case and couldn't help the tiniest prickle of disappointment when she spotted the number flashing up on the screen.

'Hey Lucy!' she said, answering the phone even as she rolled her eyes in amusement at Emmy.

'Hello lovely! Just checking in to see if you and Emmy have finished presenting your new idea to the world yet.'

'Yep. It's all up - go have a look!'

'Will do when things quieten down a bit in here - I'm behind the bar at the moment and it's gone mad.'

'Of course!' said Eve.

'Anyway - I was just calling to invite you both in for lunch - I've got a couple of the lads coming in to take over from me in about half an hour. I know Amber and Caro are busy, but Sue's going to pop in and join us if you fancied it?'

'Two secs,' she said, pulling the phone away from her ear slightly. 'Lunch in the pub with Luce and Sue in about half an hour?' she asked Emmy.

'Ooh, yes please! There's no way I can say no to a Lucy-lunch!'

Eve nodded. 'That's a yes please from both of us!'

'Perfect! We'll see you here in half an hour then.'

'Pudding?' asked Lucy as she gathered up their plates.

Eve let out a groan and rubbed her full stomach. She'd just gorged herself with her absolute favourite - a massive portion of rich, creamy lasagne.

'Not sure I've got room,' she said regretfully.

'Not even for apple crumble?'

'Okay, okay, you win,' laughed Eve.

'Pudding pusher,' chuckled Sue, handing the last plate over to Lucy with a wink.

'You love it!' laughed Lucy.

'Can't deny that,' said Sue warmly, leaning back in her own seat and taking a sip of water.

Eve watched as Lucy made her way through the packed tables towards the pub's little kitchen, and she couldn't miss the fact that Sue's eyes followed their friend all the way there too. Interesting. She'd known both of them for several years - but she'd noticed that they'd been pretty inseparable over the past six months or so.

Ever since Christmas, it was rare to bump into one without the other. She knew they'd been close for a long time, but there was something in Sue's face right now that made her wonder if there was more to it than just simple friendship.

'What's got you thinking so deeply?' asked Sue, catching her eye.

Eve jumped guiltily. Now was definitely not the time or place to broach the subject - not that it was any of her business anyway.

'Oh, you know, just wondering if this new idea's going to work out,' she said quickly.

'I've absolutely no doubt it will. You're an amazing artist, I bet you're an incredible teacher too - you're so patient. And with Emmy's social-media help combined with the village jungle-drums, I'll bet you anything you'll be booked up before you know it.'

'Thanks, Sue,' said Eve. 'I'm really excited about it now that the house is nearly ready for guests. I just need to sort out the studio a bit so that there's some indoor teaching space - and get the communal parts of the house clean and tidy.'

'Well, that won't take much - and I'm happy to give you a hand if you need help shifting stuff around in the studio?'

'Actually, that would be great. I could do with an extra bit of muscle to move the map-chest, if you wouldn't mind?'

'Of course! I've had plenty of practice - I'm sure we can handle a bit of furniture between us,' laughed Sue, flexing a bicep.

Sue worked part-time in the country store in the next town along - so not only was she a pro with a forklift, but she was also incredibly strong from humping around bags of animal feed all day. Add to that the sheer amount of digging and weeding she put into the village allotments, there was barely anything that was beyond her.

'That'd be perfect, thank you,' said Eve, gratefully. 'As long as we don't have to do it straight after pudding. I think I'd explode if we tried that!'

'How long until your first workshop starts?' asked Emmy, surfacing briefly from her own food coma.

'Two weeks,' said Eve. 'That's if I can get enough people to sign up to make it worthwhile.'

'How many spaces each week?' asked Sue.

'Six in total. And I think I'll need to have at least three to make it worth running. I really hope I fill the first one up!'

'You will! Your phone will be ringing off the-'

'Hook?' said Sue with a laugh as Eve's mobile started to vibrate on the table.

'Sorry guys,' said Eve. 'Let me just turn this . . . ooh, unknown number!'

'Answer it!' said Sue.

'At least we know it's not Lucy this time,' laughed Emmy as Eve nodded and swiped to answer the call.

'Hello, is this Eve Grey?' It was a woman's voice, but not one she recognised.

'Yes, that's me,' said Eve, suddenly feeling a bit cagey. Was this yet another scam call? She'd had so many recently - though this didn't sound like the usual opening spiel of someone trying to sell her insurance.

'I'm calling on behalf of a . . . client. We were wondering if you still have spaces available for your next art workshop?'

'You . . . you were?' Eve said in surprise. Really? The stuff had only been live for a couple of hours.

'Oh dear, don't tell me we're too late?' said the woman on the other end. 'He'll be gutted.'

'No, no, of course not. Are you okay to hold the line for just a sec while I go somewhere a bit quieter?' she asked.

'Of course.'

Eve quickly put her thumb over the microphone.

'It's someone for the course!' she squeaked at the others.

'What are you waiting for?' laughed Emmy.

'Better signal? Less noise?' said Eve desperately, eyeing the table of six behind them who were having a brilliant - if rather noisy - time of things.

'Caro's steps - round the back - just by her front door. There's great signal at the top and it'll be quieter too,' said Sue.

Eve didn't hesitate. She hurtled out of the front door and nodded her thanks to a couple of locals who hung back in the porch to let her dash past. She hurried around the back of the pub and took the outdoor staircase up to Caro's flat two at a time.

'Hello? Are you still there?' she asked, slightly out of breath.

'Yes. Everything okay?'

'Of course. Sorry - there's bad signal here in the village, I just wanted to make sure I could actually hear you,' puffed Eve, sinking down onto Caro's doorstep and hoping she didn't lose signal by doing so.

'Okay - so now that I've got your full attention,' said the woman, her voice now slightly huffy, 'there's definitely still space on the course?'

'Yes - still space,' said Eve.

'And the B&B's not booked up?'

'No - that's fine too - I've got doubles or a twin room left?' said Eve.

'Double would be great. My client has some specific requirements.'

'Oh, okay, no problem. I mean I'll do my best to-'

'He will be bringing his dog with him. I presume that won't be an issue?'

'I, err-' Eve hadn't actually given any thought to animals. In principle, she didn't have an issue with it, but it would mean having to offer it to other guests too, and warning all of them that there would be a dog present . . . but . . . this was her first booking and . . . sod it. 'Yes, that's fine. What size is he?'

'Great. He's only small. A Westie.'

Eve let out a silent sigh of relief that her house wasn't about to be taken over by a Saint Bernard.

'Now - we will need you to provide a suitable bed for Wilf.'

'The dog?' said Eve - because by this point she wasn't actually sure.

'Of course the dog,' came the huffy response. 'My client will be travelling down by train, so won't be able to bring one with him.'

'O-kay,' said Eve. This was suddenly starting to sound like one high-maintenance guest.

'My client will require a desk or a table of some sort in his room. He's a writer so will be working on his manuscript in the evenings, around the requirements of the workshop.'

'How exciting - a writer!' said Eve, enthusiastically. 'That won't be a problem.'

'Great. Two more things. Food - we will need you to cook him fresh meat for each evening meal. Chicken's his favourite.'

'And just to be clear - is this is for the dog again? Or for your client?' she asked, slightly bewildered.

'The dog of course,' the woman snapped. 'Now, for my client, you say that you provide breakfast and lunches, but as he won't have a vehicle with him, is there somewhere convenient in the village to eat?'

'There's the pub,' she said slowly. 'They do amazing food, and my guests have full use of the kitchen too. If he'd like me to get any supplies in - on top of all the chicken - I can certainly do that.'

'Perfect. Okay, one last thing - my client would be

arriving into the nearest train station. Could you possibly send me a list of local taxi services so that I can arrange a lift into Little Bamton for him?'

'Don't worry about that!' said Eve quickly. 'If you let me know the journey details, I'll be there. Call it a door-to-door service.'

She knew from bitter experience how expensive it was to get a taxi to Little Bamton, and as for public transport, sure - you could catch the bus - but only if you wanted to travel on the rare blue moon that happened on a Tuesday sometime in the leap year. Not exactly regular or reliable.

'I will let him know. Okay - so if you can hold the room, I will fill out your online booking form and sort out the payment right away.'

'Perfect!' said Eve. 'Thanks so much!' She could barely believe this was happening, and she was having a hard time stopping herself from gushing her thanks down the phone. 'Oh, before you go, can I take a name for the room, please? Then I'll know that it's your booking when it comes through.'

'Casey. Finn Casey.'

'Great. Thanks, and-'

The line went dead. Eve stared at the screen for a moment, thinking the signal might have cut out, but nope - it looked like little-miss-bossy-pants had just hung up on her. She had been about to ask if this Finn Casey had written anything she might have heard of. Maybe it was for the best that she didn't get the chance to embarrass herself by waffling even more in her excitement.

Finn Casey. She stared out at the fields behind the pub and racked her brains. Hm. He might be a writer, but not one she was familiar with. One thing was for sure, she'd be Googling her high maintenance guest as soon as she was back in front of a computer!

CHAPTER 4

*E*ve sat back and gripped the steering wheel hard to stop her hands from trembling. How on earth had this day arrived so quickly? One moment, she was getting drunk on pea-pod wine with the book club girls and talking about changing her life, and the next moment, here she was - with her life-changing!

She quickly checked her watch and then resumed her stranglehold on the steering wheel. She'd set off way too early to meet Finn - her writer guest - from the train, but she'd had so many anxiety dreams over the past week about leaving him stranded at the station that she hadn't dared to leave any later.

Sucking in a deep, calming breath, she ran through all the little last-minute jobs in her mind, ticking them off as she went. She'd bought flowers from Emmy's stall and arranged them in all the rooms. Against all odds, the course was a sell-out and she was absolutely over the moon.

On top of her mysterious writer guest, there was Cressida, a woman who would be travelling down from near London, and Betsi from south Wales. Then there were three locals - a fact that had both surprised and really pleased her. Violet had been her second booking. The sprightly old lady had explained that she was having work done on her cottage, and would love to take the workshop as well as stay with Eve for the week, so that was the last room filled.

Then there was a young girl called Scarlet who'd been in the year below Davy at school. Eve had a sneaking suspicion that Scarlet was hoping Davy might be around some of the time, and sincerely hoped that she wouldn't lose interest when she discovered that he wasn't even in the country.

Last but definitely not least was Horace, the owner of beautiful Bamton Hall. Eve had been thrilled to add him to the list as not only was he incredibly enthusiastic about the whole thing, he also offered his gardens and grounds as an additional workshop venue.

Weirdly enough, the actual teaching part of the workshop was the one thing Eve felt completely confident about. After all, she'd done it before. Art was, and always had been, her super-power and she was really excited to share it with the others.

The bit that really had her tied up in knots was the idea of playing host to all these people. Even though

Scarlet and Horace wouldn't be staying with her overnight, the other four would - and that was a big undertaking, especially when you added in Wilf the dog and his master's full-on requests. Sure, Davy had often appeared with hoards of hungry teenage boys looking for sanctuary for a weekend - but that was very different to having paying customers staying with her for a week. Yup - she was definitely pooping her pants a bit about that side of things.

She had to admit that the farmhouse was looking great. With Sue's help, she'd rearranged some of the furniture in the communal areas so that there was a bit more room for everyone to mingle if they wanted to. Then they'd managed to heave a lovely old leather-topped desk from the downstairs office up to the double bedroom she had ear-marked for Finn. If he wanted a desk, she'd give him a desk!

Eve just hoped that her weird and wonderful mix of guests would get on. Fingers crossed. Perhaps in future, she'd have the luxury of matchmaking the participants a bit more.

All in all, Eve was actually pretty glad that the day itself was finally here - she wasn't sure she'd have been able to handle any more nervous waiting!

Ah, man, would this train hurry up and arrive already?! She was going to drive herself mad worrying in circles like this!

She gave a little jump as her mobile buzzed in her pocket and she yanked it out, half expecting it to be a text from Finn to let her know that the train was delayed. It wasn't him though, it was Davy.

Hey mum, just wanted to wish you best of luck on your first day. You're going to totally rock this!! Hope one of them turns out to be a secret celeb and they tweet about it and your workshop goes viral ;) Can you imagine?! Weather here is amazing, beach is awesome. Kids are annoying! Love you, D x

P.S Can't believe you basically rented out my room as soon as I moved out ;) ;)

Eve laughed as she pocketed the phone again. Bless her boy - he'd been so excited about her plans when she'd told him on the phone. She felt the tension melt out of her shoulders slightly. If she could bring up such a loving, considerate human being, she could definitely shepherd a bunch of randoms through a week of art classes!

Aha - there it was - at last! The train drew into the station and Eve hastily hopped out of the car and made her way around to the platform to greet her guest.

'Eve?'

Ah. Okay. So this was going to be a lot, loooot harder than she'd anticipated.

She nodded, her eyes skimming over the handsome face in front of her. He was gorgeous. All tufty grey hair, his face slightly stubbly, but in a way that was definitely well-maintained rather than rampant.

'Good to meet you,' said the stranger, giving her a warm smile and holding his hand out for her to shake. 'I'm Finn. Obviously. I can't tell you how grateful I am for the lift!'

'It's . . . it's no problem,' stuttered Eve as his warm hand gripped hers for a moment.

'Oh, and this is Wilf,' he said, hoisting his smart rucksack and laptop bag more firmly onto his shoulder before gesturing down at the little white Westie who was sitting politely at his master's feet.

'Hi Wilf,' said Eve. She went to kneel down to ruffle his head, then abruptly stopped herself. 'Erm - is he . . . friendly?' she asked.

'Trained attack dog,' laughed Finn. 'Might lick you to death if you happen to have any sausages on your person, but other than that you're safe.'

Eve quickly sank down onto her knees in front of the little fluff-ball and held her hand out for him to sniff.

'Hi Wilf,' she said softly.

Wilf blinked at her a couple of times, his little tail wagging against the concrete of the platform, before he nosed the back of her hand and licked it gently.

'What a sweetie,' said Eve, delighted, as she stood back up.

'He's a little gent,' said Finn with a proud smile, and then he shook his head and let out a sigh. 'See, this is why I can never maintain an air of mystery - I go all soft over this little git and everyone knows I'm a complete pushover,' he laughed.

Eve shrugged. 'Nothing wrong with that. It's quite refreshing, to be honest.'

'By the way, I really appreciate you agreeing to Wilf coming along too. He goes everywhere with me.'

'It's my pleasure,' said Eve. She hadn't really given it much thought as she'd been too busy agreeing to everything the woman on the phone had asked - all she'd wanted was to secure her first guest. Luckily, she loved dogs.

'Are there any other animals booked in?' he asked. 'Not that it matters - Wilf will just want to be friends with everyone!'

Eve shook her head as she motioned for him to follow her out of the station towards the car. 'Not this time. Though if we decide to go up to Bamton Hall for one of the sessions, you might meet Horace's two chocolate labs. He's joining the workshop too but isn't staying over because he's so local. In his words, he "wouldn't bring those two bulldozers anywhere near a bunch of people trying to concentrate!" Anyway, this is me,' she added, pointing at her car and wincing slightly.

She was quite attached to her old car - it had seen her through several gruelling years as teen-taxi service - but now that she was about to use it to ferry a high-maintenance, paying customer around, it looked more than a little bit shabby.

'Great. Let me just grab Wilf's seatbelt harness,' said Finn, rummaging in the side pocket of his laptop bag.

Eve opened the back door for them and Wilf hopped straight in and sat perfectly still while Finn clipped him in.

'I can't believe how good he is,' she said.

Finn shrugged. 'I'd hate to have a badly behaved dog. Living in the city, it would be chaos.'

Eve nodded. She guessed he was right, but in all honesty, she couldn't imagine living any kind of life in a city. She'd been surrounded by fresh air and green fields for most of her life, and she couldn't imagine it any other way.

As they made themselves comfortable in the car, Eve realised that this had to be the best looking man she'd sat this close to in over a decade. Ah, who was she kidding? In forever! She was going to have to get past that - and quickly too! She was going to be living with the guy for the next week and teaching him and . . . sleeping in the room next to his.

Crap! Why hadn't she put him in one of the rooms down at the other end of the house?! She knew why. Because, other than her own room, his was the one with the best views and the nicest light. He was her first-ever customer to book in. She wanted his stay to be special - and not just because the woman on the phone had made so many demands that she'd been both terrified of disappointing him and super-keen that she got everything right for him. She'd always been a people pleaser!

But now, having met him, she was surprised at how easy-going he seemed - not the tightly wound, demanding client she'd been expecting.

'How far is it to Little Bamton?' he asked, making himself comfortable next to her, then glancing over his shoulder to check that Wilf was okay.

'Only about ten minutes,' she said, dragging her wandering thoughts back to reality.

'Great. Poor old Wilf will be desperate for a walk after so long on the train.'

'I bet you feel the same too!' said Eve. 'First thing I always do after a long train journey is grab a shower and then get outside in the fresh air for an hour if I can!'

'Is that a hint,' he chuckled, clamping his arms to his sides.

Eve's chest contracted as she realised how that had sounded. 'Oh my goodness, no! I'm sorry, I just meant-'

'Hey, it's okay,' laughed Finn. 'I know a hint when I hear one.'

'No really, I-'

'Can't take it back now,' he said.

Eve risked a glance in his direction and couldn't help but let a snort of relieved laughter escape at the ridiculous pouty face he was pulling.

Right - lesson number one - her mystery guest

seemed to like a good laugh. Even better, it looked like he didn't mind it being at his expense.

She had a feeling that the longer she was left on her own with Finn Casey, the more danger she was going to be in. The sooner the rest of the group rocked up, the better.

CHAPTER 5

'Right,' she said, leading the way up the staircase with Finn and Wilf following close behind. She was doing her best not to think about the fact that by going first, poor old Finn was basically being faced with a full view of her not-so-shapely derrière! Eve cleared her throat and tried to remember what she was about to tell him.

'Right?' prompted Finn. She was sure she could detect a hint of laughter in his voice.

'Yes. So - your . . . your assistant, was it, who booked you in?'

Finn snorted. 'Assistant - brilliant! Ooh, she's going to hate that,' he chuckled.

'Sorry!' said Eve quickly. 'Oh no, it wasn't your wife, was it? She kept calling you her client, so-'

'No, definitely not my wife. Heaven forbid!'

They reached the landing and Finn gave an exaggerated shudder as Eve turned to face him.

'No wife here. No girlfriend. No significant other.' He paused for a moment and let out a little sigh before hitching his smile back in place. 'I'm married to my work, and no one can really handle that.'

'So, on the phone . . . ?' prompted Eve curiously.

'That was my editor,' he said with a long-suffering look.

'Seriously?'

He nodded.

'Oh,' said Eve. Somehow she hadn't been expecting that. 'I didn't realise that they got quite so . . . hands-on?'

Finn laughed. 'Oh yes, Laura's hands-on alright. Especially when I'm late for a deadline. She'd basically do anything to get her hands on my manuscript right now, including forcing me to take an art course to get "into my hero's head-space."'

Eve's heart sank a little bit. So he didn't really want to be here. To borrow one of Davy's favourite sayings - that sucked!

'Hey, you okay?' he asked with a frown.

'Oh, sure, I'm fine. I just can't believe you've basically been *sent* here.' She'd meant it to come out as a light-hearted joke, but she'd actually managed to sound hurt.

'Don't get me wrong. Taking a course was my idea. In fact, taking *your* course was my idea. I mentioned it to her - and then the next thing I know, she's gone ahead, booked it and set everything up. She's just . . . well, she's a lot to take sometimes. I'm sure she's a great editor . . . and I really like the publisher I'm with, so I put up with it.'

Eve nodded. 'Well, I'm really glad you want to be here. Anyway, here's your room.'

She opened the door for him and then stepped aside to let Finn and Wilf pass her.

'Wow, look at this beauty!' said Finn, trailing his hand along the side of the huge desk.

'Well, it was one of your requests, so I didn't want to disappoint you!' she said.

'My requests?' said Finn, popping his laptop bag down gently onto the leather surface, then raising an eyebrow at her.

'Yeah - you know - the ones Laura gave me. A desk, a new bed for Wilf, fresh meat for Wilf that I'll cook for him for each evening meal . . .'

Finn's mouth had dropped open.

'She asked you for all that?'

Eve nodded, confused.

'And you did it all?'

'There's a tray of chicken breasts in my fridge that answers that particular question.'

'I'm *so* sorry. You must think I'm a complete diva!'

Eve grinned at him. 'Maybe a little bit . . . highly-strung?' she said gently.

'You mean spoilt?'

Eve shrugged. 'It's no problem.'

'For the record, I didn't ask for half that stuff - at least, not in that way. All I wanted was somewhere you'd be happy for me to write in the evenings, I asked if you could grab me a blanket or something for Wilf so I didn't have to bring one on the train - and a list of places I could easily grab dinner. Bloody hell, that woman! I don't know where she got the whole chicken-for-Wilf thing from. I'm so sorry for all the extra trouble.'

Eve was chuckling now. 'It's no trouble, really. Good practise for when I really *do* have a diva on my hands I guess, though I do have to admit, I did wonder if I was about to have a mystery superstar-writer on my hands.'

Finn turned away from her to take a closer look at the beautiful tartan bed she'd bought for Wilf. It was huge and squashy - way too big for the little fellow really - but Eve had figured it would be an investment for any four-legged guests that she might welcome in the future.

'Come on Wilf lad,' he said, patting the cushion. Wilf dutifully hopped in, gave a funny little sigh of contentment and flopped over sideways. 'Hmm - seems you've got his seal of approval!'

'Good. Right, I'll leave you both to settle in.'

'Also, just for the record,' said Finn quickly, 'I'm totally not a superstar writer dick. Just me.'

Eve grinned. 'And just so I've asked - your books - anything I might have read?'

Finn shook his head. 'I highly doubt it.'

There was something in his face that seemed to close up as he said this, and Eve decided to leave the poor bloke alone so he could relax a bit after his long journey.

'Tea and cake whenever you fancy it, and if you need anything, let me know,' she said, pulling the door closed behind her.

Her house was full of the sounds of laughter and chatter, and Eve had to admit that she already loved it. Horace had arrived just after she'd shown Finn up to his room, and now both Betsi and Violet were ensconced in the sitting room with him, merrily tucking into the huge Victoria sponge that Lucy had brought over that morning.

Eve had just popped into the kitchen to fill the kettle up and make a fresh pot of tea for everyone when she paused at the window. She hadn't heard Finn come back downstairs, but there he was outside, stomping up and down the path - all the way to the dry-stone wall that looked over the fields beyond, then all the way back towards the house - only to turn on his heel and do it all over again. His mobile phone was glued to his ear and there was a definite slump to his shoulders.

Eve couldn't believe that he'd actually found enough reception to move around quite so much without cutting out - maybe that's why he looked so cross? His whole demeanour had changed from when she'd been joking around with him not that long ago. Whoever it was on the other end of that call really wasn't doing his holiday-relaxation-vibes any favours.

Wilf, however, looked to be having the time of his life out there. The dog was little more than a white blur against the lush green of the garden as he dashed in ecstatic laps around Finn, giving the occasional yap of happiness. Gone was the polite dog of the train station - this was definitely Wilf-at-play!

Eve quickly ducked out of sight as Finn swung back towards the house again, his expression now thunderous. She could do without him thinking she was spying on him! Time to make the tea, head back to the sitting room and chat with her other guests.

She filled the teapot with hot water, added five cups, milk and sugar to the tray and picked it up carefully. A gale of laughter from the sitting room made her smile. It sounded like those three were getting along like a house on fire. There was just Scarlet and Cressida left to add to the mix and she'd have her full house.

Eve was just about to head out of the kitchen with the full tray in her hands when Finn burst in through the back door making her jump. The teapot and cups rattled ominously but she just about managed to save the lot before she lost her grip.

'Shit, sorry Eve!' Finn grunted, putting his hand out as if he could steady her and the tray at the same time.

'No worries,' she said, popping it all back down onto the work surface for a second. 'No harm done!'

'Don't know about that,' said Finn under his breath. 'Wilf, come here lad,' he called, letting out a piercing whistle. The little dog came galloping over, but the moment he stepped inside it was like someone had flipped a switch and he became a model citizen again.

'Such a good dog,' said Eve, shaking her head, impressed.

'Yeah. If only editors were so easy to train.'

Ah. So it was the dreaded Laura who'd managed to get him so worked up, was it?! It was on the tip of her tongue to ask him what was up, but she stopped herself. It wasn't anything to do with her.

'Fancy some tea and cake? That might help. Betsi and Violet have just arrived, and Horace is here too . . .'

'Do you mind if I take a minute?' he asked, forcing a smile. He wasn't fooling anyone though, she could see the tension around his eyes.

'Of course! Whenever you fancy. We're still waiting for Cressida and Scarlet anyway.'

Finn nodded, clearly eager to be on his own for a moment. He had an iron grip on his phone, and Eve clocked that his knuckles had turned white around it. He was holding something in - but only just.

'Can you give me a shout if I'm not down by the time the others are here and you want to start?'

'Of course,' Eve said gently, then picked the tray back up and headed out to the others. She was half hoping that Finn might help himself to a drink or something to eat before disappearing back upstairs.

If anyone asked her, he needed a break from whatever it was that was bothering him. He definitely needed a break from that editor of his. The temptation to ask more about it was huge, but she'd only met him about an hour ago. There would be plenty of time for all that later.

Scarlet and Cressida appeared at the front door at the same time as each other. Cressida, all cashmere and expensive perfume, pushed past Eve the moment she opened the door.

'Oh, erm, hi!' said Eve, stepping out of the way as fast as she could.

'Cressida Ponsonby. And I didn't realise this was a *child-friendly* week,' she sneered, throwing a look over her shoulder at Scarlet. 'Now where should I go?'

'Through to the end, there,' said Eve, taken aback that a complete stranger could be quite so rude.

Cressida disappeared around the corner, and Eve turned to welcome a very uncomfortable-looking Scarlet in.

'Is it okay that I'm here?' she muttered.

'Okay?' said Eve, smiling at her, 'are you kidding

me?! I'm chuffed you've decided to give it a go,' said Eve warmly.

Eve led Scarlet through to the sitting room and quickly introduced the newcomers to the rest of the group.

Cressida had already taken a seat at the head of the table, and Scarlet slid into the chair next to Violet. Eve couldn't help but notice that the easy banter from earlier had disappeared. Uh oh.

Scarlet was sitting with both her arms and legs crossed, doing her best to look cool and unruffled, but the waves of nerves rolling off her were a sure giveaway. She was terrified, and there was no doubt in Eve's mind that Cressida's unnecessary dig had a lot to do with that. She quickly offered her a drink and a piece of cake, but she just shook her head.

Cressida pulled a face at the cake, muttering something about "poison" and "sugar".

'I'm going to have to ask Lucy for her secret,' said Violet, a delighted look on her face as she cut another slice of sponge. 'She always manages to get it so light! I can make a decent fruit cake, but I can never get my sponges right.'

'You'd be better off with a piece of fruit,' muttered Cressida.

Violet turned to her, and without taking her eyes off the younger woman, took a very deliberate, very *large,* bite of the sponge cake.

Scarlet let out a snort of laughter, then quickly covered her face with her hands.

'Erm, okay, so I'll just go and grab Finn and then we can all get started,' said Eve, giving Scarlet a quick wink.

Eve hurried up the stairs. She was hoping against hope that this was nothing more than a few teething problems - she was desperate for the group to jell. But who really knew what was going to happen with such a mixed bunch? One nervous teenager, one reclusive writer, then there was Betsi - who appeared to be a totally chilled hippy, Cressida - who, on first appearances was auditioning for the part of the wicked witch of the group, lovely Horace who just wanted everyone to love Little Bamton as much as he did, and Violet, who was trouble - but in the very best way.

She paused by Finn's door for a second, listening before she knocked in case he was on the phone again - but there wasn't a peep from inside.

'Finn?' she said gently as she rapped on the door. 'Everyone's here if you'd like to come down and join the party?'

Finn opened the door and smiled at her, though he looked completely wiped.

'Cool, thanks. Come on Wilf!' he said, clicking his fingers. The little dog lifted his head from his bed then flopped back down.

Eve laughed. 'Bed's a success then?' she said.

'Most definitely. He's not left it the whole time I've

been up here. Come on lad!' Finn strode over to the bed and ruffled Wilf's ears, doing his best to tempt him out.

Eve couldn't help but notice that Finn had already set up the desk. There were enough bits and pieces spread across it that it looked like he'd been here at least a month already. She glanced at the laptop and spotted a Word file - open but completely blank. No hints there as to what he was working on. Damn. She couldn't help it, her curiosity was definitely on high alert!

'Right, all ready,' said Finn.

Eve blushed as he turned and caught her staring at his computer. He flashed her a tight smile and flipped the lid down.

'Just getting set up,' he mumbled.

'Of course. You know, I don't think this desk has ever seen so much action!' she said, quickly trying to cover her discomfort. 'Do you guys have everything you need up here?'

'So far,' he said. 'Right - lead the way!'

Eve hurried out of the room, getting the distinct impression she'd managed to overstep the mark. Oops.

'Sorry,' she said as Finn and a very waggy Wilf fell into step beside her in the hallway. 'I didn't mean to pry - I'm just intrigued by writers.'

Finn smiled and shook his head. 'It's fine. I'm just a bit weird about it all at the moment. I'm . . . well, I'm a bit stuck. That's why Laura called,' he paused and sighed. 'I swear, sometimes it's like we're in some kind of weird, dysfunctional relationship. I mean, I've been here what - an hour and a half? And she's already checking whether I've started writing again.'

Eve raised her eyebrows. 'That's hardly going to help.'

'Amen to that!'

CHAPTER 6

The moment they entered the sitting room, Wilf took off at a gallop and flung himself into the arms of a rather taken-aback - but thrilled looking - Scarlet.

'Hi!' she laughed as the little dog set about licking her face.

'Oh my goodness, WILF!' shouted Finn, but to no avail - the dog seemed to be in love. 'I'm so sorry, he literally never does anything like that!'

'I don't mind,' said Scarlet, who'd gone pink and was grinning at Finn over Wilf's furry little shoulder as his entire fuzzy butt waggled in time with his tail.

'Well, that's one way to break the ice,' laughed Eve as she plonked herself down in a spare chair at the table. Finn followed suit, taking the one next to her, still staring in disbelief at Wilf as he settled himself in Scarlet's lap with his head on her shoulder.

'Right, so,' said Eve, her stomach squirming with nerves as everyone turned to her. 'I know we're not really kicking things off properly until the morning, but I just wanted to give you a bit of a feel for the week, if that's okay?'

Everyone nodded, so she took a deep breath. 'Okay - tomorrow we're going to head over to the craft centre, where we're going to do a bit of preliminary work in my studio.'

'Ooh, fancy,' said Betsi.

'Well, not exactly, but it's a space where we can all have a play with some different techniques. I've set up stations around the room, so you can delve into the different mediums - especially the ones you haven't tried before.'

'What if we make a mess?' said Violet.

'That's the whole point' said Eve with a grin. 'Tomorrow is about getting a feel for things - how they behave and move. What their limits are.

'Lucy from the pub is going to bring lunch over for us, and then in the afternoon we're going to head to Grandad Jim's Flower Farm to do some sketching in Emmy's field.'

'Awesome,' breathed Scarlet, then quickly clamped her free hand over her mouth.

This prompted a round of laughter from the others, and Eve felt her shoulders drop. This was going to be okay. It might be an odd group, but they all seemed nice enough. Well . . . mostly. She glanced at Cressida's stony face and wondered if she was looking at a one-star review in the making.

'The second day,' she said, dragging her attention back to the job in hand, 'we're going up to Bamton Hall, courtesy of Horace here. There's a stunning folly, beautiful gardens, and more inspiration than you can shake a stick at.

'Day three and four will be a mixture of time spent in the studio and out and about in the village while we all work up the sketches from the first couple of days and explore how much you can develop an idea.

'Then day five . . . we will be hanging your exhibition.'

'What?' Betsi squeaked, grabbing hold of Cressida's shoulder in her excitement, only to earn herself a disgusted look as the younger woman shook her off. 'You mean, we get to put it up ourselves?' she continued, unperturbed.

'That's right! It's your work, so you're going to work as a group to curate and hang the exhibition in my studio space in time to show it off to the public on Friday afternoon and all day Saturday.'

'But everyone heads home on Saturday afternoon don't they?' said Violet, looking confused.

Eve nodded. 'You can either have your work up for sale or just show it. Anything you do want to hang in the show but want to keep after we're done, I'll send on to you when it's taken down, along with a cheque for any sales you make!'

'Amazing!' said Horace. 'It's going to be so much fun!'

'I hope you all really enjoy it - that's the whole point of this week - to explore and have fun and try new things. The exhibition is about showing off your process as much as your finished pieces - so it's definitely not something to get worked up about, okay?'

Eve looked around at them all and was relieved to see that the general reaction was excitement. Even Cressida looked like she might be thawing a bit, thank heavens.

There was just one member of the little group who was looking unconvinced. Finn had a bit of a frown going on. That said, Eve wasn't sure if he was fully in the room with them at that moment. He was glaring off into the middle-distance, and she had a sneaking suspicion he might be fretting about that phone call with Laura again.

She gave her head a little shake. 'I'm glad you're all excited. Now- I was wondering if we could all share a bit about why we're here? It would be great if we could all get to know a bit about each other.'

Eve paused and then let out a laugh at the complete lack of enthusiasm that greeted her. Suddenly everyone was more than a little bit interested in their shoelaces. 'Okay - so you're telling me I might have to rethink this bit then?'

There was a lot of awkward nodding, combined with a lack of eye contact around the table.

'You're right - it's like one of those awful team-building exercises, isn't it? Alright. Just two little questions in a quickfire round, then I promise I'll back off. Number one: your name and number two, your favourite medium to work in. Let's go this way,' she pointed to her right.

'Betsi. Wool!'

This earned Betsi a chuckle because it was pretty obvious when you looked at her that she had a wool obsession going on - her hair band, pompom scarf and jumper all looked to be hand-knitted.

'Cressida. Oils.' She gave a little sniff and looked around impressively as if she was waiting for a round of applause. It didn't come.

'Violet - and I've no idea, I've never done much like this before.'

'Ooh that's exciting,' said Eve, 'maybe you'll find a favourite this week.'

Violet's eyes lit up and she relaxed back in her chair.

'Scarlet - digital painting - if that counts?' she mumbled into the top of Wilf's head.

'Totally does,' said Eve nodding, ignoring the snort of derision from Cressida.

'Horace. Charcoal for me. Love it!'

'Finn,' said Finn, looking a bit dazed and confused. 'Erm . . . I'm like Violet, though I'm most excited to try watercolours.'

'Okay, great!' said Eve.

'What about you,' said Scarlet, surprising her.

'Oh - good point. I'm Eve - obviously - and I adore oils, and watercolours, and pastels, and pencil . . . but some days I just can't beat charcoal for the freedom.'

'Cheat,' muttered Finn with a smile.

'Yeah, Eve!' said Betsi. 'What if you could only have one of them for the rest of your life?'

Eve's jaw dropped - wasn't she meant to be the teacher here? She closed her eyes for a second, imagining all the different mediums she loved to work with. 'Okay,' she said at last, 'pencil. Because you can take one anywhere.

'Right - this next question should be an easy one. Who's ready for some food?'

Eve tried to smother a yawn as she rinsed off the last of the breakfast things under the tap. She'd made one serious oversight when she'd been preparing for having guests in her house for a week - a dishwasher! It would definitely be the first thing she changed before her next group arrived - if there was a next group.

It was definitely nice having the house full of people, but the jury was out on whether this was the way she wanted to achieve it in future. She hadn't slept much last night - the nerves had well and truly kicked in.

She turned back to the kitchen window and stared out at the garden. It was still fairly early, but her borders were a riot of colour out there in the sunshine.

She'd have to make sure she watered them before bed tonight. It looked like it was going to be a beautiful day - perfect for an afternoon of art over at Emmy's. But first things first, she had to get everyone out of the house and down to the studio.

She *had* hoped that they might all be a bit more relaxed around each other by this morning after sharing a meal at the pub last night, but it hadn't quite gone according to plan. Finn had decided to stay put at the house, opting for a sandwich in his room instead of joining them. Eve guessed he was trying to make a start on his writing, but there was a small part of her that wondered if a proper break from his laptop might be more beneficial than an evening staring at a blank screen.

Finn hadn't been the only one to opt-out. Scarlet had said her dad was picking her up early - which was a shame as Eve was pretty certain she'd texted him just to get out of any extra time spent near Cressida. But as soon as Scarlet had gone, Cressida announced that there was a wine bar more to her taste in a nearby town and that she would be driving there for her evening meal.

That had left Eve, Horace, Betsi and Violet to trundle down to the pub together. As three out of the four of them knew each other and everyone else in the village anyway, it hadn't really seemed much different to any other night in the pub in Little Bamton. Betsi seemed to enjoy herself though -

getting to know both the local people and the local ales rather well.

Breakfast this morning had been a fairly quiet affair. Scarlet and Horace were missing as they would be meeting them at the studio. Finn had appeared early and with barely a word, he'd loaded up a plate, grabbed a cup of coffee and scuttled back to his room. Eve wasn't that surprised. She was pretty sure he'd been up most of the night.

When Betsi appeared at the table, she'd looked rather worse for wear and had sat picking at the hot, buttery pastries, taking tiny sips of tea. Cressida had turned them down completely, opting instead for fruit, herbal tea and a sneer. This had left Violet and herself to carry the conversation. Eve had to admit that she'd been secretly pleased to escape to the kitchen for a while.

'Need any help?'

Eve swung around and came face to face with Finn. She couldn't help but smile at him - he clearly hadn't looked in a mirror before heading back downstairs. His hair was standing up in tufts where he must have been running his fingers through it while he'd sat working.

'I'm good thanks,' she said, trying to force her lips to behave before he thought she was being rude.

'I can't believe you're running this whole thing on your own . . .' he said, eyeballing the left-over pastries that were sitting on a plate, waiting to be emptied into a giant Tupperware in case anyone got peckish before lunch.

'Go ahead!' said Eve, gesturing at the plate.

Finn grinned and swiped a chocolatey one, looking like a naughty school kid as he bit into it.

'And, for the record,' she said, returning to his original point, 'I really don't mind running it on my own - I'm used to it. I brought up Davy, my son, pretty much sing-handedly. I've kept this place going on my own. I opened my studio on my own. In many ways, it's easier. I'm . . .' she took a deep breath, 'I'm used to it,' she said again in a quieter voice.

'Sorry - I didn't mean to pry but-'

'It's fine,' said Eve, cutting him off before things could get any more personal. She didn't much fancy having to own up to being a sad loner with no life - not on day one of her new adventure. And especially not to this guy whose tufty hair and delight over a chocolate pastry seemed to be doing something unexpected to her insides.

'So, did you manage to get some work done last night?' she asked, quickly changing the subject.

Finn nodded.

'Great!' said Eve.

Finn stared at her.

'What?' she said, rubbing her hand across her face in case she'd missed some pastry crumbs or something.

'Lies. All lies.'

'Huh?'

'I didn't. No work. I just sat there staring at the screen until halfway through the night. Then I fell asleep for a bit, but I was awake on and off. This morning, I just answered a couple of emails from Laura. That's it. That's all I've managed to do.' He let out a frustrated puff of air before tearing another bite out of his pastry.

'You've heard from her already today?' said Eve, surprised. She grabbed the dish-rag and started to run it over the surfaces so that the kitchen would be all sorted before they went out.

Finn laughed, though there wasn't a hint of amusement on his face. 'Only three emails so far.'

Eve glanced at her watch. 'But it's not even half past eight!'

'Yeah, well, that's nothing unusual.'

Eve pulled a face at him and he laughed again - at least this time it sounded a bit more natural.

'You know, I'm actually looking forward to forgetting about it all for a few hours and doing something else today.'

'Excellent!' said Eve, tossing the rag over the tap to dry. 'Shall we grab the others and get to it then?

CHAPTER 7

'Morning campers!' boomed Horace as they trekked down the driveway and turned towards the heart of the village.

'Hello!' said Eve with a welcoming smile. 'I thought you were meeting us down in the square?'

Horace shook his head. 'Beautiful morning, so I thought I'd come over early and walk down with you all.' He touched his flat cap to Betsi as she passed him - she'd clearly earned his respect when she'd sunk pint number five of the local Scabby Tabby scrumpy the previous night.

'Violet!' he said with a smile as she followed Betsi.

'Morning,' replied Violet, beetling past him.

Finn caught Eve's eye, amusement dancing there as Horace turned and fell into step beside Violet, offering her his arm - which promptly earned him a suspicious frown.

'I think he's got his work cut out with that one,' whispered Finn, as Wilf danced alongside them both on his lead.

'Oh, I don't know,' Eve muttered as Violet's laugh drifted back to them and they both watched as she looped her arm through the crook of Horace's.

'Hmm, maybe you're right. Could it be - your first workshop romance in the making?' he laughed.

'I cannot believe you expect us to walk everywhere,' sighed Cressida, clopping up behind them.

Eve glanced down, only to catch sight of Cressida's ridiculous pair of patent black, pinpoint stilettos.

'Oh, my,' she breathed. 'Gorgeous shoes, but . . . erm . . . would you like us to wait while you nip back and change them for some flats?'

'No, I wouldn't,' huffed Cressida. 'Just because the rest of you choose to look like a bunch of hairy bikers, doesn't mean I have to.'

She sped up to walk ahead of them and Eve frowned. Cressida was going to struggle when it came to Emmy's field later! Maybe she needed to amend her booking information a bit, though she could have sworn she'd put something about comfortable, sensible clothing you didn't mind getting splattered in paint somewhere in the small print.

'What?' she said, shooting a glance at Finn, whose shoulders were shaking.

'Hairy bikers?!' he snorted.

Eve rolled her eyes at him. He seemed to be lightening up with every step he took away from his laptop. Maybe this week would do him more favours than just getting inside his hero's head - if she could just prise him away from his gadgets for long enough!

The early morning summer sun was showing Little Bamton off at its very best, and as they walked past the thatched cottages, their front gardens heavy with rich summer colours, Eve felt her nerves about the day evaporate. She was in her element here. This was exactly why the village, and village life, was right at the heart of all her work. This place meant *happiness* to her. She just hoped that each of her guests would be able to tap into that feeling and take a bit of it home with them when they left.

The little group was gathered under the green willow archway in front of the craft centre, waiting for her to unlock the gates, when a voice made her turn.

'Morning Eve!'

'Hi Mark!' she said, greeting the tall man with a grin.

'First day? You've got a beautiful one for it!'

'Haven't we just?!' she said. 'Hope you'll be coming along to the grand event on Friday afternoon?'

'Wouldn't miss it for the world! Have a good day, everyone.'

'Okay . . . who was that?!' hissed Cressida in Eve's ear, her eyes following Mark as he crossed the square and headed in the direction of the church. 'Eve, was that your *boyfriend?!*'

Finn stared at Mark's retreating back and then turned back to her with his eyebrows raised.

'Mark?' Eve spluttered in surprise, then she shook her head. 'He's our vicar.'

'Oh. My. God.'

'Quite!' snorted Violet from behind her.

'But . . . he's like something out of a Mills and Boon novel!' said Cressida, fiddling with her hair distractedly.

Eve straightened up and pulled open one of the heavy gates. The whole group bundled through onto the cobbles beyond, apart from Finn who hung back to open up the other side for her.

'Hm,' he said, as he and Eve followed behind everyone else. 'So, the real question is, who's going to be the week's big scandal? I'm not so sure it's Horace and Violet after all . . . not if Cressida is planning to corrupt your vicar!'

'Shhhh,' giggled Eve, poking him in the ribs with her elbow.

Wilf chose that moment to start yapping and pulling on his lead back towards the gates.

'What? What you lunatic?!' said Finn, looking mildly concerned as Wilf ran in insane circles, trying to get the extender-lead to go further than it could.

'That's what!' laughed Eve as Scarlet strode around the corner. She broke into a grin as soon as she spotted

Wilf going absolutely ballistic at the sight of her. 'And for the record, that's who my money's on as the couple of the week,' she said, pointing as Scarlet hurried forward and dropped to her knees, Wilf climbing up onto her lap for a cuddle.

'Huh - you might just be right!'

'Okay gang! Let's get started.' said Eve as soon as they were all comfortably ensconced on high plastic stools in her light, bright studio. She'd purposefully cleared the space of all her own work, not wanting to sway anyone in any particular direction. She wanted everyone to really explore their own passions when it came to making art this week.

'We've got charcoal, pencils, pastels, watercolour, acrylic and pen and ink set up,' she said, pointing out the six different stations around the room. 'I want all of you to spend some time at each station. This is going to be like the art-supply version of speed dating - you'll get about twenty minutes with each.'

'But what are we going to paint?' asked Scarlet, looking around.

'Nothing in particular!' said Eve.

'Oh, that *does* sound useful,' scoffed Cressida.

'Sounds like someone's *scared*,' smirked Violet, much to Eve's surprise - though the rest of the group looked delighted.

'As if!' spat Cressida, flushing.

'Well, erm . . .' Eve stuttered, trying to get herself back on track and doing her best to ignore the squabbling. 'This bit is about getting the feel for whatever you're working with - pushing it to its limits - so I actually *want* you to make a mess. See how much paint you can put on a piece of paper before it's too much and starts to disintegrate, how hard you can lean on charcoal before it breaks, how dark and light you can go with the same pencil - you get the idea?'

She looked around, glad to see most of them nodding, though Cressida was still looking decidedly sulky.

'Now - I know it's human nature to go straight to the thing you feel most comfortable with - so instead, I want you to try something that's out of your comfort zone first!'

'That's probably charcoal for me,' said Betsi, 'Messy and monotone -about as far from wool as I can get.'

'Great!' said Eve, encouragingly. 'Horace?'

'Hm. Acrylics I think.'

'Okay, Finn?'

'No idea,' he said.

Eve turned to him and was surprised to see he was looking mildly terrified.

'How about watercolour - as that's the one you want to explore?'

'Okay,' he said, and wandered over to that station.

'I'll take pastels if that's okay?' said Scarlet.

'Sure! Okay, Cressida and Violet - you two have got pencil and pen to choose between.'

'I don't mind starting with either. What would you like?' said Violet, raising her eyebrows at Cressida. The words might sound friendly enough, but the look on her face certainly wasn't.

'Fine. Pencil then.'

'Great. I will take pen and ink, Eve.'

'Okay everyone - ready to see what these tools can do? Get to your stations . . . and off you go!'

Eve blew a whistle - which had seemed like a bit of fun when she'd come up with the plan, but in this small space, it was a bit like a gun going off. Several of them jumped, and then all of them started to laugh. Well - that was definitely one way to break through the nervous tension!

Eve gave everyone a few minutes before setting off on a lap of the room to see how they were getting on.

'Okay?' she asked Scarlet. The young girl was already absorbed, trying out colours in great big swirls on the paper in front of her. Scarlet nodded, not taking her eyes off what she was doing.

'Don't forget you can use the broad edge of the pastel too, and have a play with blending them - there's a box of tissues there if you want to use them - loads of people use their hands too . . .'

Hands it was. Scarlet started to work the red and orange patches together with the side of her fist, and then let out a huge sigh.

'I keep looking for the undo button when I don't like something,' she laughed.

'Eh?' said Eve, looking non-plussed.

'Like with the digital painting - if you don't like something, you can just take it back a step. This is so different. You kind of have to be . . . braver?'

Eve nodded, excited that Scarlet had already come across something quite so profound within her first couple of minutes. She moved on, not wanting to put her off.

Betsi seemed to be having a grand time with the charcoal, playing with long dark lines and tiny little feathery strokes . . . that looked suspiciously like wisps of wool. Eve smiled to herself. It looked like you might take the knitter away from her wool stash, but she'd still find a way back to it.

Cressida had grabbed a 2B pencil and rather than trying anything playful, she was making a tiny sketch of a vase of flowers in one corner of her piece of paper.

'Lovely - next, why not grab one of the really soft leads and go big - just to get a feel for the difference?' suggested Eve.

'But I've not finished this, yet!'

'Totally up to you,' said Eve quickly, not wanting to push her too soon.

'Am I doing this right?' laughed Violet.

Eve turned to check out how Violet was getting on with her pen and ink. She hadn't been sure what she'd expected to see, but it wasn't this. Violet had already covered her sheet in quirky caricatures of them all - working away with brushes in hand.

'Wait a minute, we've got a ringer on our hands!' laughed Eve. 'I thought you said you'd not done any kind of art before?'

Violet shrugged. 'I haven't, not really. My old dad used to draw with me on school holidays but that was . . . sixty years ago, maybe?'

'They're beautiful,' said Eve, looking more closely at the wonderfully playful, loose lines.

'Oh don't, you'll make me blush,' chuckled Violet, nudging Eve in the ribs.

'I'll leave you to play,' said Eve, moving on to Horace, who had about as much paint on his shirt - and even a splodge on his cheek - as there was on the paper in front of him.

'Kind of thick, this stuff!' he said with a grin.

'And very fast drying. That's why I like playing with it. Unlike oils, where you have to wait for days between layers, you can work much faster with these - and there are loads of things you can add to the paint too - to make it thicker, thinner, gritty . . . you name it! But if you want it to move a bit easier, try mixing a touch more water with the paint.'

Eve moved on to Finn and peeped at his sheet. He glanced up at her and then stepped back a bit. Considering he was working with watercolours, his page was curiously tidy - and almost empty. In his hand was the smallest brush available, and he'd used the minimum amount of water on the paint pans, transferring the colour into tiny, intense blocks of colour on the paper. It was almost like he was trying to make the least mess and remain as invisible as possible.

'It's a great way to see the colours on the paper,' said Eve, diplomatically. 'I often do that when I get a new set or new colours to work with.'

'I don't really know what I'm doing,' said Finn, sounding nervous.

Eve picked up one of the large, round brushes that were great for making great swathes of colour in lush washes because they greedily sucked up water and pigment. She held it out to him, and Finn took it, looking like it might bite him.

'Add loads of water and get splattering!' she said with a smile. 'See how far you can make the colours travel - and what happens when you drag one wet colour into another.'

Finn took the brush and nodded, dunking it carefully into the water glass. He peeped up at Eve again, who nodded encouragingly. As soon as he looked down at the paper again, she decided to wander off and let him explore without her breathing down his neck.

Before long, she gave the whistle another blast as a signal for them all to stop what they were doing.

'Two seconds breather before you switch to your next station!' she said. 'If you can take your work and pop it on the bench at the back?'

Everyone did as she asked, casting curious glances

at each other's work while she whizzed around, set out new paper and freshened each station up for the next session.

'Alright everyone - shift one station clockwise, and off we go again!' said Eve, blowing her whistle as everyone scrabbled into their new positions.

As they did so, Eve drifted over to where they'd set out the first session's work. As her eyes travelled across them all, she paused on Finn's page. A full set of tiny coloured boxes and one wide, tidy stripe of blue down the side of the paper. Hmm. Maybe it wasn't just words that Finn was stuck with?

By the time they'd all visited each of the six stations, everyone looked knackered - but mostly happy. Eve knew that it had been quite a challenge for most of them, but she'd noticed that by the third change, they'd all loosened up considerably, experimenting without worrying too much about the outcome.

All of them, that was, apart from Finn. He just didn't seem to be able to let loose and enjoy himself. Interestingly, the charcoal station had seemed to be the hardest for him - but she couldn't decide if that was because he simply didn't know what to do with the messy, tactile willow sticks, or because his phone had started to vibrate with an incoming call as he'd sat staring at the blank piece of paper.

Finn hadn't actually answered the phone - she had to give him that - and had quickly turned the vibration off so that it wouldn't disturb any of the others. Even so, she'd seen the screen light up several more times, and each time he froze, staring at it until whoever it was gave up. Maybe she should say something to him about it - for his sake. No, she couldn't, could she? It was only the first morning. She'd keep an eye on things and only say something if she really had to.

'Well done everyone!' she said after blowing her whistle for the last time. 'Excellent work this morning, I hope you've all enjoyed experimenting!'

There were cheers and nods, and Eve was thrilled to see that even Cressida was looking flushed and happy.

'Now, it's time for some-'

'Lunch!' called Lucy from the door, as she backed into the studio carrying a large tray.

CHAPTER 8

'Was it something I said?' said Lucy, plonking the huge tray of hot pasties, plates, knives, forks and serviettes down on one of the tables near the door and staring after Finn who'd disappeared outside the minute she'd arrived.

Eve quickly shook her head at Lucy and then turned to the rest of the group. 'Tuck in, everyone!' she said, before drawing her friend aside under the cover of much excited chatter and pasty-munching.

'Definitely not you, don't worry. His phone's been going all morning,' she muttered, staring through the window at Finn, who had his mobile glued to his ear. His frown was firmly back in place and he was doing the funny kind of dance that told her he was desperately trying to find enough signal for an actual conversation

'Hope it's not bad news,' said Lucy quietly. 'Looks like it might be.'

'I think it *is* bad news - and her name is Laura.'

'Wife?' asked Lucy.

'His editor. Total nightmare from what I can gather.'

'Huh, so he's single then?' said Lucy.

The sudden change of subject threw Eve for a second. She frowned at her friend. 'Yes - he is, not that that makes any difference to anything. He said he was married to his writing. He clearly doesn't have the time or the energy to focus on anything other than books.'

'We'll see,' grinned Lucy. 'Don't underestimate the healing power of hanging out in Little Bamton for a few days. Anyway, that reminds me!' she paused and, reaching into her pinafore dress pocket, pulled out a chunky paperback and handed it to Eve. 'I chose this for the next book club read. I forgot to tell everyone the last time we met up - what with all your exciting plans!'

Eve flipped it over and squealed in excitement. It was the fourth book in FC Chase's wildly popular *Indulgence* series. They'd already flown through the first three gorgeously steamy romances, but had been trying to hold off before reading this instalment because the final book of the series - book five - had been postponed by the publisher. Again.

'Oooh - is that the most recent FC Chase?' said Betsi, brandishing her half-finished pasty at Eve.

Eve nodded. 'We've been reading the series in our book club.'

'Isn't it *gorgeous?!*' she said. 'I've read all of them so far. Can't wait for the last book to come out.'

'I'm dreading getting to the end of this one!' said Lucy.

'Why?' said Betsi. 'No spoilers, but it's brilliant.'

'What if she never finishes the last one?! Can you imagine!'

'Don't say that,' squeaked Betsi, pouting. 'She's my favourite, I'd be gutted!'

'Why?' said Cressida, moving towards them. She was carrying her pasty on a folded serviette and had yet to take a bite. 'I mean, they're hardly high-literature. What's the big deal if it never gets finished?'

Violet mouthed the word *snob* behind Cressida's back, forcing a laugh out of Lucy which she quickly tried to mask as a sneeze. 'Just going to grab pudding,' she muttered, scuttling back outside.

'It would be awful if she abandoned the series,' said Eve, hugging the book to her. 'I love these characters!'

'What I'm *saying* is, even if she didn't finish it, it would hardly leave a gap in the history of literature, would it?' Cressida paused, took a sniff of the pasty and pulled a face.

'Use it or lose it, Cressie!' said Betsi, waving the last bit of her pasty at Cressida and eyeballing her own untouched one hungrily. 'These beauts are divine!'

'It's *Cressida*. And hands-off,' she said, nibbling at one corner.

Betsi smirked at her.

'Well,' said Eve, trying not to laugh as Cressida started to inhale her pasty, 'I think we're going to have to agree to disagree on this,' she said, stroking the book's cover and wishing she could disappear for an hour to binge-read the first few chapters.

'Disagree on what?' said Finn as he reappeared in the studio, flashing Eve a quick smile as he held open the door for Lucy, who had already returned bearing another tray of food.

Eve waved her book at him.

'What the hell's that doing here?' he grumbled, his face dropping into a scowl.

Lucy raised her eyebrows in surprise.

'We're reading it for our next book club,' said Eve, grabbing her handbag from under one of the tables and stashing the paperback carefully out of sight. Who'd have thought that one little book would elicit quite so much attention?!

'Well . . . I'd have thought you'd have gone for something a bit more worthwhile,' muttered Finn.

'Exactly what I said,' nodded Cressida.

'What rubbish,' said Violet, turning away from Horace, who she'd been deep in conversation with at the back of the studio. 'Have either of you even read them?' she demanded turning to Finn and then Cressida, who both shook their heads. 'Those books are wonderfully written - funny, insightful. You know, you can miss out on an awful lot of things by turning your nose up at them before you've even tried them,' Violet paused and stared at Cressida. 'Enjoying your pasty?' she asked pointedly.

'What do you think, Scarlet?' said Horace, addressing the teen who was sitting on the studio floor, her back against the wall with Wilf curled up against her side. She paused in the act of feeding the little dog a lump of steak from her pasty and shrugged.

'Whatever gets people reading has got to be good, right?' she mumbled, looking mildly horrified to find everyone's attention on her.

'Well said!' nodded Horace.

'I just wish she wasn't such a mystery,' sighed Betsi.

'What do you mean,' demanded Finn.

Eve turned to him with her eyebrows raised. Whatever that phone call had been about must have really worked its way under his skin. Where had the jokey guy from this morning gone?

Betsi didn't seem to take any offence though. She just shrugged. 'Well, she's really private, isn't she? FC Chase, I mean. She's on social media but never posts anything personal, just book-related stuff. There's no profile photo, just a graphic. I reckon it's just someone from her publisher behind those accounts.'

'What difference does that make, though?' he said.

'Well, it *would* be nice to be able to connect with her more personally. I started the series to take my mind off things when my husband was ill,' she paused a moment. 'Her books were there for me when he died. At times, they were the only things that got me through the day. Losing myself in her stories was the only way I could escape from all the shit that was going on. She was the first person to make me smile again. I just wanted to be able to tell her that.'

'Oh, Betsi!' said Horace looking devastated as he patted her shoulder gently.

'I'm okay!' she said, turning to smile at him. 'But that's what I meant about her being a mystery. I wanted to get in touch with her. I did send her page a message on Facebook - and I even wrote her a letter and sent it to her publisher.'

'Did you ever hear back?' asked Lucy, looking intrigued.

Betsi shook her head. 'It wasn't about that though. I just wanted her to know that she was making a real difference to people.'

'I . . . I never thought about it like that,' said Finn, a definite catch in his voice. 'I'm so sorry, Betsi!'

She shook her head, waving away his apology.

'Well, you never know,' said Violet, piping up again. 'The press is always speculating about who she is, maybe you'll get your wish and find out one day - they're bound to catch her out at some point!'

'I hope not!' said Betsi, looking horrified. 'At least, not like that!'

'Imagine, you might have already met her and not even know!' said Eve.

'Yeah right. About as likely as flying pigs,' muttered Finn. 'Excuse me,' he added as his phone lit up again, and he hurried back outside in search of a decent bit of signal.

There was an awkward silence for a moment, filled only by the contented sounds of Wilf snaffling the last bit of Scarlet's pasty crust.

'Aaaaanyway - chocolate brownies!' said Lucy, breaking the tension. She stepped forward and whipped the gingham cloth off the top of the newly arrived tray with a flourish. 'Complete with ice cream - so you'd better get in there quick!'

The afternoon was an absolute scorcher, and Eve was incredibly grateful to lead the group out of the studio, which had started to feel like a bit of an oven by the time they'd all finished lunch.

They ambled together towards Grandad Jim's Flower Farm on the other side of the village. Emmy had been delighted when Eve had asked if it would be okay to bring everyone over for an afternoon of drawing and painting in the fresh air.

There was a very lazy feel to everything, and Eve was more than happy for the group to take their time to stop and admire the gorgeous gardens and green, rolling

Devon hills and valleys beyond. The hedges that lined the little stream that trickled alongside the road were buzzing with life, and the hazy, sultry heat - combined with a belly full of ice cream and chocolate brownie - were making her more than a little bit snoozy.

Wilf seemed to be having the same problem, and every time Finn paused, the little dog would flop down in the shade, panting.

'Poor lad,' laughed Finn when he did it for the third time in as many minutes. 'You're wanting your afternoon nap after all that stolen pasty!'

'Well, there's plenty of long, cool grass he can crash out in when we get to Emmy's,' said Eve.

'I think I rather fancy joining him!' said Finn, a weary look on his face.

'Didn't you sleep well last night?' asked Eve in a worried tone. 'Is there anything you need to make your room more comfortable?'

Finn shook his head and smiled at her, although it didn't really reach his eyes. 'The room's perfect. It's just me. I haven't slept properly for ages.'

'Well, hopefully all this fresh air will help,' said Eve gently.

'Be nice if it did,' he sighed, glancing yet again at the screen of his phone.

Eve watched him for a moment as he bent to tickle Wilf behind the ears. She had a sneaking suspicion that Finn might sleep better if someone confiscated that phone of his . . . and his laptop!

The rest of the group had caught up now, and they all plonked themselves down on the low stone wall of the double hump-back bridge at the junction that led up to Emmy's.

Horace patted the spot of wall next to him, and Violet promptly hopped up and turned to smile at him.

Eve's heart squeezed at the look that passed between them, and she wondered for a moment if their little joke this morning about a workshop romance might just come true.

'Oh my goodness - look at these!'

Eve's attention snapped over to Cressida, who was standing in front of Emmy's flower stall, looking delighted.

'Gorgeous, eh?' she said, smiling to see her usually stroppy guest looking genuinely happy about something for a change.

'Aren't they just?' said Cressida, reaching out to stroke the petals of a deep pink rose.

'Well, thank you very much!' came a cheerful voice as Emmy strode into view, a galvanised bucket under each arm bearing a veritable waterfall of colourful blooms. 'For that, you can have first sniff of these!' she said, holding one of the buckets up to Cressida's face.

Cressida looked taken aback for a moment but then leant forward and inhaled.

'Heaven,' she sighed, a smile creeping across her face.

'Roses and lavender and sweet peas and phlox and ..'

'Watch it,' laughed Eve, standing up to greet her friend, 'when this one starts listing flowers, there's no stopping her!'

Emmy stuck her tongue out at Eve, plonked the buckets down next to the stall and turned to give her friend a rather grubby, hot hug.

'Everything's all set up - easels and drawing boards in the spots we discussed. And your boxes of supplies are by the potting-bench, so you're all ready to rock.'

'You're an angel, Emmy. You didn't need to do all that!' said Eve gratefully.

Eve had stashed everything she'd need for this session in Emmy's little potting shed a couple of days earlier. They'd decided that it would be far easier than trying to lug everything over at the same time as shepherding her guests - something she was now incredibly grateful for, given the heat.

'So, how's it all going?' asked Emmy quietly, as everyone else wandered over towards the cart to take a closer look at the flowers.

'Pretty well. Definitely some ... erm ... interesting characters!' laughed Eve.

'Violet causing trouble as usual?' chuckled Emmy, who had a soft spot for the old woman after she'd made her feel so welcome when she'd arrived in the spring.

Eve shook her head. 'No - she's mostly behaving

herself - though I think her mind's on other things right now, if I'm honest.'

'Renovations at her cottage?' asked Emmy, her voice full of sympathy. She knew how much the improvements had been worrying her prickly friend - mainly because her boyfriend, Jon, was involved in re-doing her kitchen and bathroom for her.

Eve shook her head. 'It's not that,' she whispered. She gave a subtle nod to the cart, where Horace was busy lifting down a posy of sweet peas and lavender and presenting it to a blushing Violet. He then quickly pulled out a five-pound note and popped it into Emmy's honesty box.

'Well I never,' breathed Emmy, giving Eve's hand an excited squeeze.

CHAPTER 9

Peace seemed to have descended upon the little group as they all settled down in different spots around the field. A few of them had decided to shift around from where Eve had originally planned, and she wasn't surprised to find Violet and Horace had gravitated towards each other. They were now working within chatting distance, although they seemed to be more than happy to sketch in companionable silence.

The task for the afternoon was simple - find something that caught their eye and get it onto paper - in whatever way they chose.

Eve had brought her own sketchbook, and in between checking on the others she'd decided to sketch the group at work. It was a challenge for her - she didn't often include people in her pieces, and it felt good to be pushing herself as well as her students.

After focusing on her page for half an hour, making little studies of each of them, Eve stood up, stretched and went on a quick tour to check everyone was doing okay.

Scarlet was playing with pastels again and turned to greet her in a cloud of coloured chalk.

'This is so cool,' she said.

'I'm so glad you're enjoying it! May I take a peek?' asked Eve. She made it her policy to approach from the front and ask permission before looking at her students' easels - this stemmed from a long-held hatred of tutors sneaking up and criticising work when you were at your most vulnerable.

'Sure!' said Scarlet. 'Do you mind if I go for a bit of a walk, my arm's going numb!'

Eve nodded. 'Go for it. It takes some time to get used to working standing up like this.'

Scarlet nodded. 'Yeah, but my eyes don't hurt like they do when I've been working on my tablet too long!'

She ambled away in the direction of the little river at the side of the field.

Eve moved to look at her work and smiled. Scarlet clearly had some real talent. She'd been sketching one of the vibrant growing beds, but the way she'd used the pastels made the flowers look like some graphic components from a computer game. It was fresh and unusual, and Eve found herself hoping that Scarlet might like to sell this one in the exhibition at the end of the week - because if she did, she'd buy it and frame it as a gift for Davy.

Eve peered around at the others, and her eyes paused on Finn. He was watching Scarlet as she passed under the low, leafy branches that grew beside the river. Eve chuckled as she spotted a little white fluffball following her. Yet again, Finn had been abandoned by his faithful hound as Wilf went in search of his new playmate.

She made her way over towards him and he greeted her with an eye-roll.

'Alone again. I'm starting to get a bit of a complex here,' he said with a laugh.

'How are you getting on?' asked Eve.

Finn's smile dropped and he shrugged.

'Can I take a look?' asked Eve.

'There's not much to look at.'

Eve moved around the easel and stared at the large, empty piece of paper. Then her eye came to rest on his mobile phone that was propped up next to it.

'What did you choose to work with?' she asked curiously.

Finn held out a pencil and waggled it at her.

'Not paint?' she asked. 'I thought you'd be getting into that hero's head and splashing away with the watercolours!'

Finn shrugged again, a guilty look crossing his face. 'I was going to but then . . . I don't know . . . this felt safer.'

'And?' she said.

'And I don't know where to start,' he huffed, clearly frustrated with himself.

'What were you focusing on?' she said.

Finn shrugged for a third time, reminding Eve forcibly of Davy in one of his rare stroppy-teenage moments.

'No wrong answers here, Finn,' she said with a gentle smile.

'I don't know. Some of the time I was watching you work. Some of the time I was watching Horace and Violet.'

'But what were you thinking about drawing?' she prompted.

'I . . . I wasn't. I was just daydreaming, I guess.'

'Okay, well . . .' Eve wasn't quite sure what to say. She didn't mind people daydreaming. In fact, it was something she actively encouraged. But she got the impression that Finn wasn't really being truthful. She'd spent quite a bit of time watching each of her students in turn as she tried to capture them in her sketchbook. She hadn't seen any evidence of Finn looking around as he'd claimed. In fact, most of the time, he'd been hunched up tightly behind his easel. Then it dawned on her - he'd been staring at his phone.

'Can we try something?' she asked him.

'Of course,' he nodded.

'Do you trust me?' she said.

'Of . . erm . . . of course,' he said again, more hesitantly this time.

'Gee, thanks!' she laughed.

Finn had the good grace to look a bit sheepish. 'Of course I do,' he repeated in a firmer voice.

'Great!' said Eve, and then before he could say anything else, she swiped his mobile phone and pocketed it.

'Hey!' he said in surprise.

'I'll give it back later. I promise.'

'But-'

'Finn - there's barely any signal down here. You're not going to be able to talk to anyone anyway.'

'But-'

Eve just shook her head. 'Nope.

Finn took a deep breath in and then blew it out through pursed lips, making a frustrated sound. For a second, Eve wondered if he was about to blow his top, then he gave her a defeated look.

'Okay. Fine,' he muttered.

'Good. Now then.'

Eve bent down to the supplies box she'd put together for each of her students and quickly pulled out a set of watercolours and an empty jar, poured water into it from a little bottle and then grabbed the largest brush she could find.

Finn watched in complete confusion as she mixed up a well of verdant green, followed by a second one of purple, and a third of yellow. Then she took a sheet of watercolour paper and pinned it to the drawing board in front of him.

'Take this,' she said, brandishing the brush at him.

Finn did as he was told, looking mildly terrified.

'Close your eyes,' she said.

'Sorry, what?'

'Close. Your. Eyes.'

'O-kay,' said Finn.

Eve watched him closely as he closed his eyes. Then he just sat completely still in front of his piece of paper, holding his brush.

'Do you mind if I touch you?' she said.

'I . . . erm . . .' Fin spluttered, half in amusement, half in horror. 'No, that's fine,' he finally managed to choke out.

Eve was intensely grateful that his eyes were closed as her face did a super-nova blush at his reaction reaction. She really should think of a better way to ask that particular question in future.

She stepped up behind him and coming to rest beside his shoulder, reached out and wrapped her right hand around his.

She felt Finn take a shaky breath. For a second she just stood there, wondering what on earth she was thinking, putting herself in this position. Surely he could hear how her heart was pounding in double-time? It felt strangely intimate - but it wasn't as if she could back away now, was it? Anyway, he needed this - and if she could help him break down these walls he seemed to have put up around himself, then it was her job to try.

Eve gently guided his hand towards the mixed pool of green paint, then caught the flutter of his eyelashes.

'Oi - no cheating,' she said quickly. 'Keep 'em closed!'

Finn chuckled, and she felt him relax a bit as he did as she commanded. Eve helped him to clumsily dip his brush into the paint, and watched as the bristles greedily sucked up the pigment.

She slowly guided his hand back towards the easel, and then her instincts took over. Eve forgot all about the weirdness of the situation as she glanced past the easel at the graceful curve of the flower stem she'd chosen to focus on. As her eyes travelled its length, she guided Finn's hand in a wide, winding sweep of colour on the page. Moving in shorter, sharper motions, she added movement and colour.

As she worked, she could feel Finn giving in to the experiment. It was like he was slowly learning to trust her. His muscles started to uncoil, and he followed her movements - not in surrender - but in some kind of strange duet.

Eve guided his hand back to the side, helping him plunge the brush back into the water. Swirling it around, she watched as the pigment uncoiled from the bristles and swam in the water.

Together, they scooped up some yellow, added petals, and dotted highlights into the wash of the background. Eve watched in delight as the paint journeyed into the wet parts of the paper. She never got tired of the magical dance of watercolours.

She chanced a look at Finn's face, and her breath caught. The frown had gone and a contented smile seemed to be tugging at the corners of his mouth.

'You've stopped,' he breathed.

'We've stopped,' she corrected, cringing as her voice came out in a bit of a croak.

'Can I look?'

'Sure,' said Eve, then realised she was still standing pressed against him, her hand still covering his.

She let go of him quickly and stepped back as Finn opened his eyes. He stared at the sunshine-filled painting he'd just been a part of, and then he turned, his eyes locking on hers.

'Okay?' she asked after a long, uncomfortable moment.

'Okay,' he said, and the smile finally took over his face.

Eve swallowed and took another step away from him, feeling the void between them like some kind of physical wound. Maybe she was a bit too hot, or needed a drink or ... something.

'Hey, Eve?' he said, not taking his eyes off her.

'Yeah?'

'Can I get my phone back now?'

Eve rolled her eyes, feeling the strange moment between them break.

'Fat chance.'

'When then?'

'Do me some paintings - then we can talk,' she said, forcing a smile and finally turning away from him. 'I'm just going to grab a bottle of water.'

She was in desperate need of a cold drink, though perhaps a cold shower might be more appropriate right now.

CHAPTER 10

*E*ve sat on the edge of her bed, fiddling with her phone. She'd just finished chatting with Davy. She had hoped that hearing his voice would help calm the chaos of nerves that had been swooping through her since returning from the flower field, but if anything she felt even more unsettled.

Davy was having a brilliant time. As she'd listened to him wax lyrical about the beautiful buildings, playing in the sea with his brothers, and hours spent bonding with his father and his step-mother, a heavy sense of loneliness had settled on her chest again.

Sure, she might have a house full of giggling guests, and she'd be lucky to snatch more than a few moments peace before the end of the week, but it wasn't the same. She felt Davy's absence like a soul-deep ache.

Weirdly, that strange moment down in the flower field with Finn hadn't helped matters. She'd only done it to try to help him, but that physical contact seemed to have scrambled her insides. Sure, he was attractive. Really rather hard to keep her eyes off in fact - but this was about more than that. The moment she'd taken his hand she'd had this strange sense of everything falling into place. It felt . . . right.

There was something magnetic about Finn, and she wanted nothing more than to get to the bottom of the mystery of what was holding him back.

No. No - that was the last thing she needed. Hadn't she told the girls the whole point of these weeks was that they were very light on both commitment and complications?

Eve stood up abruptly and went to stare out at the garden, which looked like it was glowing in the last of the day's light.

She knew she was a coward - but when they'd finished the afternoon's session, she'd sent everyone off to the pub for a drink and bite to eat while she'd stayed behind to pack everything up. When she was finished, Eve had sent Lucy a text asking her to let everyone know that something had come up. Then she'd put her tail firmly between her legs and retreated back to the Farmhouse to make up all the bedrooms and then hide. Pathetic. Completely pathetic. But she had to get her guard back up otherwise she was going to be in real trouble.

They were all off up to Bamton Hall in the morning, which was perfect. There would be plenty of space and plenty of distractions. She'd just have to make sure that she kept her attention firmly on the others and avoid any more intimate hand-holding with the mysterious Finn Casey.

Eve was just drawing her curtains and considering sneaking into bed early when a knock at the door made her jump.

She quickly ran her hands through her hair before going to open it. She stepped back abruptly as soon as she spotted Finn standing there, a lazy smile on his face.

'Hey!' he said.

'Oh, Finn . . . hi! Erm, everything okay?'

'I was going to ask you the same thing,' he said, cocking his head. 'Just wanted to check you're okay - we were all a bit worried. Hope nothing bad happened?'

Eve took a deep breath. Great, now she was worrying her guests because she was a neurotic mess. Not exactly ideal!

'Thanks Finn,' she said, smiling at him. 'I'm fine, really. I just had a couple of things crop up that I had to deal with.'

'Oh, right . . . okay.'

For some reason, he was looking unconvinced.

'Then I had to sort out the rooms and speak to Davy . . .'

'How's he getting on? Everything okay?'

'He's doing great, thanks. Having a brilliant time.'

Damn. She'd felt her smile slip as she'd said that. She quickly crossed her arms and hitched her professional face back in place. 'So - if there's nothing else I can do for you?' she said, moving forward in an attempt to signal that the conversation was over and she'd really rather like to go to bed now.

'Actually, there is,' he said, raising his eyebrows and grinning at her.

Eve's heart rate instantly sped up. Oh hell. Something inside her - something that felt decidedly like an uncontrollable, randy teenager - had woken up, and it was busy telling her that now would be the perfect time to launch herself at this poor, unsuspecting guy.

'Uh-huh?' she managed to choke out.

'My phone?' said Finn. 'You disappeared with it in your pocket earlier.'

It was like a bucket of cold water landing on her head. His phone. Of course.

'That's if my paintings lived up to my side of the bargain?' he asked with a mischievous look on his face.

Eve nodded and retreated to where her jacket was hanging over the back of her desk chair and reached for the phone which was still in her pocket.

She straightened up, only to find Finn standing right next to her.

'Thanks,' he said, as she placed the mobile in his hand. 'For what it's worth - you were right.'

'Right?'

'I've had a much better afternoon without this,' he

said waggling the handset at her.

'Good, I'm glad,' she said tightly. She was aware that she was sounding cold, dismissive even, but right now she was struggling to catch her breath properly. She could feel the waves of summer warmth radiating from him. She cleared her throat. 'Well - I'm always here to kidnap your phone when you need me to!'

There, that was better. She sounded a little bit less like a robot. She pushed her hair back behind her ears and smiled up at him, half expecting him to turn and leave now that he'd got what he came for.

Instead, Finn reached out and touched his index finger to her cheek. Eve froze as the tiny, warm contact sent a tingling sensation through her skin.

'Paint,' he said with a smile.

'Oh.' She wasn't quite sure what else to say.

'I'd better . . .' he waved his phone at her again, paused for a long second and then turned on his heel and headed for the door.

The moment it clicked closed behind him, Eve headed into her en-suite and looked in the mirror. Sure enough, there was a large green fingerprint on her cheek - the exact colour she'd used with Finn. She quickly grabbed her flannel, ran it under the cold tap and continued to scrub her face long after all the paint had disappeared.

She'd been wrong. Tomorrow was going to be a nightmare.

. . .

Eve let out a huge sigh and slumped back on the picnic blanket. She'd managed to hold it together for most of the morning by sticking with her plan of spending more time with the others and giving Finn a bit of space. But it had really taken it out of her.

She quickly sat forward again and started to gather together the remnants of the feast Lucy had put together for them. Sue had turned up with it at precisely the right moment, and Eve made a mental note to make sure that she roped Lucy in on a more formal basis should she ever decide to repeat the insanity that was this week.

Considering it was only day two, and her nerves were already shot to pieces, Eve had to admit that she was questioning whether it was a good idea after all. That said, her students seemed to be having a grand time today - Cressida included.

Violet had confided to Eve over breakfast that she'd walked in on Cressida with her nose in a book the previous evening, and she was almost certain that it had been the first book in the FC Chase series. She wasn't one hundred per cent sure though, because Cressida had promptly stuffed the book down the side of her chair when she realised that she had company.

Eve glanced around her now, wondering where she'd got to. Horace had taken Violet and Betsi off for a little tour of the rose gardens, Scarlet had asked Finn if she could take Wilf for a paddle in the stream that meandered through the lower stretch of the formal gardens, and Finn . . . well, Eve had done her best not to follow his every move. Still, she'd somehow managed to notice that he'd wandered off in the opposite direction to the others, his phone clamped to his ear again.

She sighed and clipped the top onto the leftovers of a huge potato salad. To give him his due, Finn hadn't touched his phone while they'd been working that morning - which was a huge improvement on the previous day. Still, there was a part of her that wished he'd just left it behind at the farmhouse - but of course he hadn't. She just hoped that whoever he was talking to now didn't ruin the rest of the day for him.

Gah! She had to stop obsessing about Finn! Even when she was actively avoiding him, it seemed he managed to worm his way into her thoughts. She wouldn't admit it for the world, but after his visit to her room the previous evening, her dreams had been full of his eyes and his hands and his-

'Need a hand?'

The blush started somewhere in the bottom of her feet but only took a couple of seconds to wash right over her. She turned awkwardly and looked up at the figure standing over her, silhouetted against the blazing blue summer sky. There they were - the eyes that had haunted her all night.

'I'm good thanks,' she said, her voice coming out tight and embarrassed. 'I'm nearly done.'

'In that case . . .' Finn dropped to his knees next to

her on the blanket and started gathering up the last bits and pieces, placing them in a neat pile inside the cardboard box she'd been using to gather everything together.

'Thanks,' she said. 'You know, you don't need to - you should be having a break before this afternoon.'

'You too!' said Finn, shrugging. 'Anyway, I hardly feel like I've had the chance to see you this morning.'

Eve felt a guilty knot form in her stomach. Sure, she *had* been trying to limit the time she spent with him for her own sanity - and for the sake of trying to remain professional after what had felt like a couple of *decidedly* personal encounters the day before - but she really hadn't meant for him to notice. In fact, it was a bit of a disaster that he had. It wasn't his fault that her innerteen was getting out of control.

'I'm sorry,' she said. 'The morning flew past. I'm not quite used to making sure I get around to everyone in each session.'

Finn sat back and peered at her for a second. Eve felt her blush intensify. Ah crap.

'You don't need to apologise!' he laughed. 'I think you're an amazing teacher - if that's worth anything. You really helped me yesterday, taking that phone away . . . getting me to lighten up a bit.'

'Great. Great . . . and thanks,' said Eve distractedly, tugging at the corner of the blanket until he scooted off the edge so that she could fold it and add it to the top of the box.

'Right, that's that done,' she said, and then mentally kicked herself. Could she please stop herself from coming out with any more inane mutterings around this guy?

'Great!' he said, picking up the box before she could object. 'Now, tell me where you want this.'

'It's okay, I can-'

'Don't argue,' he said. 'Besides, I've got an ulterior motive. I've got a favour to ask.'

Eve swallowed. Favour. Uh oh!

She led him over to the shady porch of the little folly where Sue had asked her to leave everything when they'd finished. Sue was planning to whisk Lucy away from the pub for a walk around the gardens this afternoon, and planned to pick it up at the same time. Once again, Eve wondered what the story was with her two friends. Maybe she was just imagining things because of how she was feeling herself.

One thing was for sure, if she didn't manage things a bit better around Finn this afternoon, she'd be calling an emergency book club meeting - not for the bookish gossip - but for some advice on how to avoid jumping on the poor bloke before he managed to escape at the end of the week.

Eve shook her head and suddenly realised that she was gazing at the rather pleasant sight of Finn's bum as he bent to set the heavy box down against the old stone wall.

'Penny for them?' he said, straightening up to stare at her.

'Oh - nothing,' she said quickly. Caught in the act! She *had* to get a grip. Mmm. A nice firm grip.

Oh heaven help her!

'Just thinking about the afternoon session, that's all,' she replied in a strangled voice.

'You know,' said Finn with a frown, 'you look like you might have had a bit too much sun.'

'Yeah. You might be right,' she said, covering her burning face with her hands for a moment, grabbing the ready-made excuse.

'Right, I've got an idea,' he said. 'First, get this down you!' He leaned forward and plucked one of the small, unopened bottles of water from the picnic box and handed it to her.

Eve smiled at him - he really did seem to be a nice guy. She dutifully cracked open the top and took a sip, even though she'd been mainlining water all morning. Better that he thought it was the sun rather than anything to do with his rather shapely bottom.

'Good. Right, are you feeling up to a short walk?'

'I'm fine, really-' She was going to make her excuses about needing to start rounding up the others, but he cut her off.

'Great. Let's go down to the river. I need to free Scarlet up from Wilf-sitting duties, and you look like you could do with a paddle.'

'Oh, I . . .'

But she was too late. Finn had already started to walk in the direction of the stream. Eve let out a breath, then reluctantly turned to follow him.

They walked in silence until they reached the river, then paused in a shady spot under the branches of a leafy old oak. It was a beautiful spot, and Eve felt some of the tension leave her body in spite of herself.

'Damn!' said Finn.

'What's up?' she asked in surprise.

'I thought Wilf and Scarlet would still be down here.'

'I really wouldn't worry,' said Eve. 'They've probably gone on an adventure.'

Finn scratched his nose. 'I feel a bit bad, lumbering her with Wilf - but I needed to make that call, and-'

'Finn, I really don't think you need to worry - at least, not about those two. I might not know much about dogs, but I do know teenagers - and they always turn up when they're hungry!'

Finn chuckled. 'Yep - just about covers it for dogs too - but they've only just had lunch!'

'Rule number two about teenagers - they're nearly *always* hungry. Anyway - all joking aside, Scarlet loves Wilf - she won't mind.'

'Yeah - you're probably right.'

'Shall we-'

'Let's paddle anyway!' said Finn, a grin spreading over his face as he dropped to sit on the grass and started to remove his boots and socks.

'I'm good thanks,' said Eve.

'Don't be a party pooper,' he laughed, and there was something in his face that reminded her of Davy when he was little. That pure, boyish excitement. Without saying anything, she plonked her bum down beside him and started to take her trainers off.

'That's my girl,' said Finn.

Something pleasurable wiggled in Eve's stomach, but she didn't dare think about it too much. The sensible part of Eve's brain was screaming at her to stop and go and find the others, but her inner-teen was telling her to have some fun. That voice was a lot, *lot* louder.

Finn got to his feet, and before she knew it, her hands were in his as he helped her up.

She quickly let go, trying to ignore the fact that all the hairs on the back of her arms were standing on end in spite of the heat of the day.

They picked their way carefully down the bank and Finn splashed straight into the water, letting out a huge sigh of relief.

Eve followed him in a bit more gingerly. The water wasn't deep, and as it washed over her hot feet and swirled around her ankles, she couldn't help the huge smile that spread across her face.

Sunlight was dancing on the rippling water, sending glimmers of gold rippling across her toes. Eve closed her eyes for a moment, letting the sounds of birdsong and the splashy, playful stream wash away everything else from her mind.

'Better?' asked Finn.

She opened her eyes only to find him watching her with a soft smile on his face.

'Much. Thank you,' she replied truthfully. 'Oh, what was that favour you mentioned?'

Finn grinned and bent to swish his hands in the cool water. 'Nothing major,' he said, looking back up at her. 'Just wondering if you'd mind confiscating my phone again this afternoon?'

Eve let out a surprised snort of laughter.

'Turns out I'm a fan of being bossed around. Well . . . by you at least,' he amended.

'Oh,' said Eve, feeling a little spike of nerves again. 'Of course - no probs. Hand it over!' she said, holding out her hand.

'Now?'

'No time like the present!'

'Oh, okay, fair enough.' Finn went to straighten up but only made it half way before the stones shifted under his feet. He let out a grunt as his footing shifted and he flung his arms out in a desperate attempt to right himself.

Eve sprung forward and managed to catch hold of one of his hands, steadying him for a second - but it was too late. With a gasp, Finn started to topple backwards, pulling her with him.

Eve let out a squeal as they both splashed down into

the water, Finn landing flat on his back with her thumping down on top of him.

She quickly raised her face from his soggy chest to stare at him. 'Are you okay?' she demanded, struggling to sit up without kneeing him anywhere sensitive.

'Well,' he said, sounding a bit winded as he angled his head to look at her, 'that's one way to cool off.'

Eve spluttered and gave in to a wave of giggles as she watched the water dripping from his hair.

Finn scrambled to sit up, and Eve, scuttling like a crab in order to get to her feet, held her hand out to help him. She wrapped her fingers around his and yanked, pulling him to his feet, then steadied him with one palm against his chest.

'Um,' said Eve, suddenly hyper-aware of his heartbeat and the warmth of his hand in hers. They were so close she could see tiny droplets of water clinging to his eyelashes. All the laughter was gone from Finn's face now, and his eyes were locked on hers.

For just a moment, everything around her stilled, and all Eve could think about were the silver flecks in his eyes, and whether he was about to kiss her.

'Oi!' Cressida's shout from the bank made them both jump guiltily apart. This time it was Eve who nearly tumbled back into the water.

'Are you going to *bother* teaching us anything this afternoon, or are we just paying to watch you two canoodle?'

CHAPTER 11

'Finn? Your clothes are dry,' said Eve, approaching him quietly.

He looked up and smiled at her. In the hour since they'd been back from Bamton Hall, Finn had set up a kind of make-shift office out here. The little wrought-iron table, which sat at the very end of her garden, now held several notebooks and his laptop.

Wilf, who was ensconced in the shade underneath the table, lifted his head from his paws and gave her a brief wag of his tail before flopping back down. Scarlet had clearly managed to wipe the little lad out.

'Ah great, thanks so much!' said Finn.

After their dunk into the river, they'd both headed back up to the rest of the group, avoiding eye contact with each other as well as Cressida, who was acting as a highly grumpy chaperone.

Eve had managed to escape too much of drenching,

given that she'd landed on top of Finn, and the damp patches on her clothes had started to dry before they'd even reached the others.

Finn, however, was another matter. He was soaked through. Eve could only imagine the water had made it all the way through to his pants - though she was doing her best to keep her mind firmly away from Finn's pants. Sadly, her best was proving to be rather lacking.

As soon as they'd reached the others, Horace had come to the rescue and had whisked Finn inside the Hall to dry off. He'd lent him a change of clothes and Finn had spent the afternoon looking like some strange 1920s throwback - sketching away on the lawn whilst wearing a pair of smart linen trousers and a striped grey and red shirt. It should have made him look ridiculous, but Eve had struggled to keep her eyes off him all afternoon.

'I'm, erm, I'm really sorry about your phone,' she said, popping the folded clothes down on the table next to him. 'Don't suppose the rice worked?'

Finn shook his head. 'Nah, I reckon it might be a goner. Don't worry about it - it's no one's fault!' he said quickly, spotting the look on her face.

Finn's phone had been in his trouser pocket when he'd landed in the river. After they'd both got back onto the warm, grassy bank, Finn had dragged it out only to find that it was completely dead. Horace had packed it into a Tupperware box full of dry rice in the hope it might help.

'Maybe it's a good thing,' she said tentatively. 'At least it means you might get a bit of peace while you're here?'

'Yeah. Chance would be a fine thing,' muttered Finn.

'What do you mean?'

'I've had five emails from Laura since I checked earlier. Five. And now she keeps trying to get me on messenger too.'

'But . . . if she keeps distracting you every time you sit down, how does she expect you to get any work done?!'

'Good question,' he sighed.

'I thought you'd come out here to make a start,' said Eve, giving him a sympathetic glance.

'I had. Being outside all afternoon up at the Hall got all these ideas going in my head. But then I opened this bloody thing and there were all these suggestions and questions and demands and . . .' he paused. 'I'm just stuck again. Sorry, you don't need to hear all this. Part of me wishes the laptop ended up in that river too, though. I just need a bit of peace, you know? I need to be left alone for a bit.'

Eve flinched. She was pretty sure he was only talking about Laura's incessant demands, but nevertheless - he could probably do without her turning up and interrupting every time he sat down to work.

'I'll leave you to it,' she said quietly.

'Eve - I didn't mean you!' he said, his voice urgent.

She turned back to him and gave a shy smile. 'I

know.' She'd love to sit down opposite him, flip closed that laptop and find out a bit more about this man who was quickly taking up residence in her head. But he needed some space. And anyway, she'd just come up with a plan that could really help him out. 'Give me a shout if you need anything.'

Eve hurried back towards the house. Other than her and Finn, only Cressida was at home. Horace had invited everyone to stay for an evening meal at the Hall. Both Violet and Betsi had jumped at the idea, and Horace had talked Scarlet into staying too, promising everyone a ride home in his Rolls Royce after they'd eaten.

But Finn had admitted that he really needed to do a couple of hours of work, and Cressida had been adamant that she wanted to come back to the B&B as well. With two of her guests headed home, Eve had also declined the invitation. It had everything to do with being a good host - and absolutely nothing to do with Finn. Nope. Not one little bit.

Eve paused at Cressida's door, then knocked quietly.

'Yeah?' came a muffled voice.

'Can I come in a sec?' shouted Eve.

'Oh. Um - okay.'

Eve heard some rustling and then Cressida opened the door, blocking her view into the room.

'Yeah?' she asked again.

Eve couldn't help but notice that her eyes were a bit pink. Had she been crying? 'You okay?' she asked gently.

'What? Oh yeah, fine. Hay fever,' she said shortly, rubbing her eyes.

'Oh. You poor thing,' said Eve. 'Do you need anything?'

'I'm sorted.' Cressida shook her head. 'Thanks,' she added as an afterthought.

Eve looked at her a moment longer. Hay fever? Cressida hadn't sniffed, snuffled or sneezed the whole time they'd been out in the gardens. That said, she had to admit that she'd been pretty caught up in her own thoughts all afternoon, so she could have easily missed it.

'So - what was it you wanted?' Cressida asked, sounding impatient.

'Oh . . . just checking if you're using the Wifi? It's a bit glitchy so I was going to turn it off for a bit to see if I could get it to reboot.'

Cressida shook her head. 'Nope. Thanks for checking though. I'm going to go down to the pub for some food, so I'll be out of the way.'

She raised her eyebrows at Eve significantly, and for a moment, Eve wondered what she was missing. Oh no, did she think . . .? Gah, awkward.

'I-'

'Catch you later.' Cressida abruptly shut the door in her face.

Well, at least that made things more simple. Eve hurried back down the stairs, let herself into her office and promptly turned off her wifi hub at the wall. There. If Finn needed peace and quiet, she'd give him peace and quiet.

She headed back out into the kitchen, popped the kettle on and then went to look out at the garden - peering in Finn's direction. Sure enough, he had a look of confusion on his face. He closed the laptop lid, opened it again, hammered at the keyboard for a moment, swivelled the whole thing around on the table to look at the back and then leaned back in his chair, gazing aimlessly around the garden.

Hm. Maybe it hadn't been such a great idea after all. Perhaps she'd take him a cup of tea, tell him she'd had to reboot and then switch it back on. But as she continued to stare out of the window, waiting for the kettle to boil, something happened.

Finn gave a little shrug. Then he stretched his arms over his head, straightened his back in the chair . . . and started to type.

Maybe her little ploy was working after all.

'Bollocking bollocking bollocks!'

The sounds of Finn's frustrated cursing drifted through her bedroom wall, and Eve put down her book with a frown. Should she go and check he was okay? Or was that just ridiculous?

About an hour ago, Finn had come in from the garden with Wilf at his heels and his laptop under his arm, muttered something about mosquitoes and working upstairs, and then had disappeared up to his room.

Cressida had turned up from her meal at the pub shortly afterwards and headed up to her room too. Then, just twenty minutes ago, Betsi and Violet had rocked up, giggling like a pair of schoolgirls.

It transpired that Betsi had been telling Violet all about Bridgerton, and they'd begged Eve to use her Netflix account. Eve had readily agreed, flicked the Wifi back on, and left the two women cosied up in the living room, tucking into a family-sized bag of crisps and the delights of the delicious Duke.

With an unexpected evening free, Eve had hurried up to her own room, keen to make a start on her much-anticipated book club read. FC Chase was one of her favourite writers, and she'd quickly pulled on her PJs, thrown herself on top of her duvet, and dived into the first chapter with a contented sigh.

It hadn't taken very long, however, for her to become aware of the sounds of agitated pacing coming from next door.

'Seriously, bollock off!' came another muffled curse.

That was it. She didn't know what was going on, but she was going to have to check everything was okay.

She quickly grabbed a hair-bobble and popped it

into her book so that she didn't lose her page, then headed for the door.

'Finn?' she said softly, knocking lightly on his door.

There was a little *wuff* from Wilf, a quick scuffle, and then Finn appeared.

'What's up?' he asked, a look of surprise on his face as he took in her flannel PJs and bare feet. Eve instantly wished she'd had the presence of mind to at least pull a cardigan on.

'Erm - I just - I wanted to check everything's alright,' she said.

'In your pyjamas?' he said, quirking a smile.

'Well . . . yes! I heard you through the wall. I just wanted to . . . to check.'

'Ah hell, I'm so sorry Eve. I didn't realise I was being that loud.'

Eve quickly shook her head. 'Don't worry about that - as long as you're okay?'

'I'm fine,' he said, with a quick shake of his head.

'Well . . . if you're sure . . .' she said, unable to keep the scepticism out of her voice. She took a step back from the door. Time to retreat. 'Sorry to bother-'

'It's bloody Laura,' he burst out, flinging the door open wide and beckoning for her to follow him in.

She hesitated for just a moment, and then followed him reluctantly. She'd had a hard enough time today trying to stop her overactive imagination from running away with her when it came to Finn. Being in his bedroom seemed to be asking for trouble.

'What's she done?' she asked, watching as he plonked himself down on the edge of the bed. She leaned on the hard back of the desk chair, not quite knowing what to do with herself.

'She. Just. Won't. Stop!'

Eve bent down and scruffed Wilf behind the ears as he wandered over to greet her, his tail going into overdrive.

She smiled as Wilf seemed to grin up at her, then glanced up only to find Finn staring. She straightened up quickly, realising that her PJ top might not quite be offering the . . . support . . . she could really do with in this situation.

Eve cleared her throat and as Wilf headed back towards his ginormous bed.

'I don't get it,' she said at last, breaking the awkward silence that had descended. 'You seemed to be going great guns out in the garden earlier?'

Finn shrugged. 'I don't know - something must have happened to your internet - maybe I was just too far down the garden for it to work or something. Anyway, it cut out right in the middle of her messaging me. And . . . it was like this massive weight was lifted. I managed to get some words down for the first time in ages - that's why I didn't stop to chat when I came back in. I get lost in it when it's going well - and for the first time in ages, it was. I was all excited to come up here and carry on.'

'That's brilliant!' said Eve, though she had a

sneaking suspicion that she knew what was coming next.

'Yeah. It was brilliant!' he said. 'But about ten minutes after I came up here, I guess I managed to reconnect or something because the wifi kicked back in and all these emails and messages started coming through. It sounds so stupid - but it was like they just blocked the words up again.'

'Ah. I'm sorry.'

'Me too. It sucks. Anyway - I'm really sorry. I didn't mean to disturb you with my rubbish. I'll keep it down, I promise.'

'It's fine, really!' said Eve again. 'And by the way - it isn't rubbish. Can I . . . no, don't worry.' She turned towards the door.

'What?' said Finn, watching her curiously.

Eve turned back to him. 'Can I ask you something?'

'Of course!'

Deciding to be brave, Eve made her way over and perched beside him on the bed. Finn looked mildly surprised but didn't protest.

'Well, why don't you just turn your wifi off?' she asked.

'Fair question - you're going to think I'm really stupid.' He leaned back and, grabbing one of the squashy pillows, hugged it to him.

Eve practically melted. The unguarded moment made her want to wrap her arms around him. 'I'm really not, I promise,' she said.

SUMMER NIGHTS AND PILLOW FIGHTS

'I can't. As in - I know how to turn it off, but - I can't. Not when I know that she's there - sending all these emails and messages and they're just going to be there waiting for me when I turn it back on.'

Eve nodded. 'But earlier, in the garden?'

'That was different. It was out of my hands. Nothing I could do about it. Like when you confiscated my phone,' he said with a smile.

'Yeah.' She paused. 'And like when I turned the Wifi off at the mains.'

Finn gaped at her.

'I just wanted to . . . see,' she said with a guilty look at him.

'Unbelievable,' he said, a look of complete surprise on his face.

'Well - I guess it worked,' she said with a smirk. A reckless, naughty mood was coming over her. What was it about this man that seemed to be bringing out this side of her she thought was long gone? 'You know, there *is* an answer to all your problems!'

'Oh yeah?' he said, his lips tugging up into a playful smile. 'And what's that, huh? Live off-grid?'

Eve shook her head. 'Well - I've successfully destroyed your phone. I could always confiscate your laptop too?'

Finn let out a bark of laughter. 'Unbelievable!' he said again, then grabbing his pillow, he swiped it at her, catching her by surprise.

'Oh no you don't!' squealed Eve, scrabbling backwards, grabbing his other pillow and swinging it around to connect with Finn's head.

'This means war young lady!' he grunted, pummelling her again and again, the pillow flying from all sides until she collapsed backwards on the bed, giggling for mercy.

'*Young lady,*' she spluttered as Finn collapsed back next to her and they lay staring at the ceiling. 'It's been a very long time since I've been called that!'

They peeped sideways at each other, and as their eyes locked, the giggles melted away.

Was he going to kiss her? Eve held her breath. He *was* going to kiss her. Or at least, if she stayed here, drowning in his eyes for a second longer, she was going to kiss him.

Eve quickly scrambled off the bed, turning back to him, only to find a confused look on his face as he followed her more slowly.

'I've got an idea,' she said as he got to his feet.

'Eve-?'

'Come through to my room a sec,' she said and hurried out of the room.

'Eve, what-?'

'Come in! Give me a sec,' she said, going over to her wardrobe and pulling open the door. She rummaged behind the shoeboxes standing in neat rows at the bottom and then felt the plastic handle she was hunting for. With a grunt, she lifted the heavy case out from behind everything else and turned to set it down on her bed.

Finn, who'd been hovering awkwardly by the door, came over to stand near her.

Not daring to look him in the eye again for fear of melting into a puddle, she unzipped the case, loosened the clip and flipped the top back.

'Wow,' said Finn. 'I wasn't expecting that!'

They both stared down at the beautiful curves of a vintage, sea-green typewriter.

'It was my grandmother's. It works perfectly.'

'But - I don't get-'

'I *am* going to confiscate your laptop. This is the replacement,' she said, turning to look at him at last.

Finn stared down at her, then back at the typewriter, then back to her again, a slow smile appearing on his face.

Eve couldn't take it any longer. She reached up and planted a soft kiss right on his smiling lips.

'Sorry!' she said, stepping back like she'd been burned.

'Eve-'

Finn reached out and caught hold of her hand, drawing her slowly back towards him. He brushed her hair back behind her ear and, tilting her face back up to his, he kissed her hard as he wrapped his arms around her.

CHAPTER 12

'Need a hand with that?' Finn's voice whispered right in her ear, almost making her drop the water jug she'd been filling as he circled his arms around her waist and pulled her back to him.

'Oi, behave!' she giggled as he kissed the back of her neck, trying to swat him away without slopping water down her front.

'I wouldn't have got up so early if I'd known there was a ban on canoodling in the kitchen,' he chuckled.

'You didn't need to get up early, but I've got to get the breakfast table ready. Anyway, don't you think we did enough canoodling yesterday?'

'Are you kidding me? Not nearly enough!' he said, taking the jug away from her, setting it down on the side and drawing her towards him again.

Eve gave in with a sigh and sank against him. Last night had been . . . amazing, and crazy, and unexpected.

It had been midnight when she'd finally kicked him out of her room. Every molecule of her being had wanted him to stay - but a little voice in her head had told her to go slow. Or at least slower than she wanted to. She'd only met the guy a few days ago and things were . . . complicated. Or maybe they weren't. Maybe this could be a simple, lovely, uncomplicated thing. Who was she kidding?

'The table's ready for the others. Can't we just have breakfast in bed?' he said with a suggestive wiggle of his eyebrows.

'Mr Casey, is that any way to talk to your teacher?'

'No Miss,' he pouted, making her laugh.

'Good. Anyway - I wanted to get the typewriter set up for you before the others come down.'

Finn sighed. 'Actually, that would be great.'

In between snogging like naughty teenagers the night before, Eve had offered Finn the use of the desk in her downstairs office. If he was going to use the typewriter to tackle his book, he needed to be somewhere where he could clatter away without the fear of disturbing anyone else. Eve's study was perfect as it was it was well away from all the communal areas and a good distance from the bedrooms too. As far as she was concerned, it was his until he left at the end of the week.

'You okay?' he asked, watching her.

'Of course,' she said, quickly hitching her smile back in place.

Thinking about the end of the week had just given her an unexpected stab of pain. Was it just yesterday she'd been daydreaming about having the place to herself again? Things looked very different this morning - she was really going to miss everyone. And when she said everyone, of course - she meant Finn.

'Alright, out with it!' he said, grabbing her hand.

'It's nothing, just . . . I was just thinking about the end of the week - and you going back to London.'

'Looking forward to seeing the back of me already, eh?' he said with a smile.

She shook her head. 'Exactly the opposite,' she said, embarrassment lacing her words. 'Sorry, I know I'm being stupid.'

'Hey! No you're not! For what it's worth, I don't like thinking about it either. Especially not after last night. Not with - well - with whatever this is,' he said, lifting her hand and kissing the back of it.

Eve leant forward and gingerly ran a finger down his cheek. 'I know . . .' she said in a whisper.

Finn leaned forward and kissed her gently.

'Well well well! *Someone* had a good evening then?'

Eve and Finn jumped apart looking guiltily around, only to come face to face with a very mischievous looking Violet standing in the doorway.

'How long have you been there?' said Eve indignantly, her face heating up uncomfortably.

'Long enough to feel like I can give you some advice,' she said. 'Get that kettle on girl.'

Finn quirked an amused eyebrow at Eve, who quickly turned to refill the kettle.

'Now then,' said Violet, easing herself into one of the kitchen chairs. 'You two were carrying on like you'd never see each other after the end of this week.'

'You really were standing there quite a while,' laughed Finn. 'Enjoy the show?'

'Don't flatter yourself, young man - it was hardly Bridgerton!'

Eve snorted in spite of herself.

'All I was going to say was - just get on and enjoy yourselves. That's what Horace and I are doing.'

'You and Horace?' said Finn. 'Ooh, more workshop gossip!'

'Do you want this advice or don't you?' she demanded, glaring at him.

Finn grinned back. 'Sorry. Go ahead.'

'Too kind,' she said, raising an eyebrow. 'Now what was I saying? Ah yes, just enjoy your time together! Don't worry about the end of the week or what's coming next. In this day and age, if you wish to start a relationship, the trifling matter of living at either side of the country is hardly going to stand in your way, is it?'

Eve turned to look at her and cocked her head, about to argue.

'Don't give me that look, young lady. With all this modern technology, and sexting-'

Finn snorted and Eve's eyes were suddenly out on stalks. 'Violet!' she said in horror.

'Don't *Violet* me!' she huffed. 'If only there'd been this much fun to be had when I was young! Anyway. That's all. Have fun and don't start worrying about how the next bit will pan out. If it's meant to be - it will be.'

'Erm, thanks for that!' said Finn, his shoulders still shaking with barely suppressed laughter.

Eve nodded and handed Violet a cup of tea. 'Yeah, thanks,' she said, secretly wondering how long it would take for her to get the idea of Violet and Horace sexting out of her head. 'Can I ask one thing,' she added, catching Violet's eye.

'Of course. But if it's how to sext, you're probably better off asking Scarlet - or your son.'

'What?!' spluttered Eve, at exactly the same time Finn let out a great honk of laughter.

'Oh, you know - these teens . . .' she said vaguely.

Eve shook her head, desperately trying to get her thoughts back on track. 'No . . . no . . . I was just going to ask if you'd mind keeping this quiet?'

'And by this, you mean-?' said Violet.

'Me and Finn!' she clarified.

'Really?' said Finn, looking a bit crestfallen.

'You've never been on the receiving end of the Little Bamton jungle drums!' she sighed. 'Nothing personal - it's just new, and a bit scary and . . .'

'And she'd rather not spend the next three months

being asked questions about it in the village pub,' Violet finished for her.

'Exactly,' said Eve, looking at her with pleading eyes. 'So, will you, Violet.'

'Okay - but it won't help.'

'What do you mean?' said Finn, looking perplexed.

'There's already a sweepstake going on whether you two'll get together by the end of the week!'

'Yep - and by the looks of things, I'm owed some money!'

All three of them span around to find Betsi standing in the doorway, wearing a long knitted nightgown and a wide grin.

Eve stood at the end of the pub garden and stared out across the view of the gently rolling fields that seemed to be rippling in the summer evening heat. She was glowing - and it wasn't from a whole day spent teaching in the sunshine. Nor was it because something had clicked with her little group today while they'd all explored the art of keeping a sketchbook.

No, this deep sense of excited, happy anticipation had come from every secret look and stolen touch she'd shared with Finn as they'd ambled around the fields and lanes of Little Bamton.

She knew she should have been focusing on the day's workshop - but seeing Finn engrossed in the pages of his own sketchbook, and catching him watching her while she was showing Scarlet and Cressida how to make a spread more cohesive - had worked some kind of strange magic on her. Put it like this - she had a feeling that she was going to find it a *lot* more difficult to keep things slow between them when they were finally alone again.

'Here ya go. Refill!'

Eve turned away from the view to find Caro standing next to her, holding out a glass of chilled white wine.

'Oh, you angel!' said Eve. 'You finished behind the bar for the day?'

Caro shook her head. 'Just grabbing a quick breather. What are you doing out here all on your own?' she said, watching Eve closely.

Eve took a quick sip of her wine to buy some time and looked back out at the view again. She'd decided to join everyone for a drink at the end of their afternoon session. The others were all engaged in a wonderfully rowdy game of darts in the bar - but she'd just needed a moment alone.

She caught Caro's eye, and her friend quirked an eyebrow, clearly still waiting for an answer.

'I kissed Finn,' she blurted.

'Nice!' said Caro, chinking her glass against Eve's.

'Is that all you've got to say?' laughed Eve.

'What do you want me to say - that I *told* you so?!' chuckled Caro.

'You did not.'

'Did too. I said you'd end up indulging in a bit of student-teacher sexy-times if you started these workshops, remember?'

Eve snorted. 'Oh god, I do remember. That was after you polished off Sue's pea-pod wine wasn't it?!'

'Don't remind me,' laughed Caro. 'Anyway, I'm chuffed for you. It's obviously doing you a ton of good - your eyes are sparkling and you're all . . . glowy!'

'Thanks,' said Eve, taking another sip of wine to avoid looking at her friend.

'So I ask you again - why are you hiding out here when the guy with the *decidedly* tasty derrière is in there getting whooped at darts by a teenager?'

'I just needed . . . a second. Just to figure it out,' Eve mumbled.

'What's to figure out?' said Caro. 'He's hot. I'm assuming he's single? And he's clearly potty about you!'

'He is at least two of those things. Jury's out on the third. But . . . I live here, he lives in London. What about the future?'

'You're over-thinking,' said Caro.

'Yeah, ya think?' said Eve with a laugh. 'I just haven't done this in a really long time. It wasn't in the plan.'

'Take it from me - it's simple.'

'Huh. Right.'

'It is. Do you like him?'

'Yup.'

'Does he like you?'

'Seems so.'

'Then stop worrying about everything and just enjoy yourself.'

'That's what Violet said,' huffed Eve.

'You told *Violet?* Are you *mad?*'

'She overheard us talking. Anyway, she promised to keep it quiet . . .'

'You'd have more luck keeping it quiet by skywriting it over the village square,' laughed Caro.

'You're a real comfort, you know that, right?' said Eve, wrapping her arm around her friend.

'I try!'

'Eve?'

The girls whipped around to find Finn strolling towards them.

'Oh, hey Finn,' said Eve with a smile, uncomfortably aware that she was blushing. 'This is Caro.'

'Nice to meet you,' said Finn with a smile.

'You too! You're Wilf's dad, right?'

Finn nodded. 'Yep, that's me.'

'Where is Wilf?' asked Eve, looking around for the little furball.

'He's off for a sleepover at Scarlet's!' he said. 'She begged hard enough that I caved!'

'Aw - that's so cute!' said Caro.

'Yeah. Well - actually, it's kind of handy. I need to get some work done this evening. Eve, sorry to be a pain, but I was wondering if you would mind giving me a hand to get started with the typewriter in a bit?'

Eve nodded. 'Of course.'

'Typewriter?' said Caro.

'Finn's a writer.'

'Oh, cool - but you work on a typewriter?'

'Long story,' laughed Eve, draining the rest of her wine. 'But it involves me confiscating his laptop.'

'O-kay then,' said Caro, looking confused. 'You two kids have fun! I'd better get back to work anyway.'

They said their goodbyes to Caro and then, rather than going back through the pub, Eve led Finn around the side in the hope that they didn't draw too much attention. As soon as they were out of the square, Finn reached for her hand and laced his fingers through hers.

Eve's stomach did a little somersault and she smiled up at him.

'You know I've used a typewriter before, right?' he said as they strode back in the direction of the farmhouse.

'Oh. Okay, so-' she paused in her tracks.

'So I'm all set up in your office and good to go. I just wanted to get you on your own for a while,' he said, smiling down at her.

Eve grinned at him. What was it Caro had said - stop worrying about everything and enjoy herself?

'Come on,' she said, tugging at his hand. 'Haven't I got a laptop to confiscate?'

CHAPTER 13

*E*ve woke up and stretched. Her room was pitch dark. She grinned to herself, safe in the knowledge that no one could see her face, and curled her toes in glee. Well, she'd certainly followed Caro's advice to the letter. They'd definitely had fun.

She turned over and reached her hand out to where Finn was sleeping - only to find an empty stretch of cold mattress beside her. She couldn't believe it - had he really gone back to his room after she'd fallen asleep?

She flipped on the bedside light and peered around as her eyes adjusted. Nope - there was no sign of him.

Eve rubbed her face. She could either turn off the light and go back to sleep . . . or find out where he'd got to.

She quickly got to her feet, pulled on a robe and grabbed her little torch from her bedside table - no point waking everyone up by switching lights on. The last thing she wanted to do right now was answer any awkward questions.

Not that any of the others were likely to be awake. They'd all sounded fairly merry when they'd finally rolled in from the pub. She and Finn had had to smother their faces in the pillows to stop their giggles from escaping when they'd heard Betsi and Cressida staggering along the landing, singing a particularly filthy rhyme, with Violet bringing up the rear and repeating just the rude words at the top of her voice.

Eve padded over to the door and cracked it open. It was long past midnight and the hallway was pitch black and deserted. She could just about detect a snuffling snore drifting down the corridor from the direction of Cressida's room. Eve bit down on a smile - Cressida might be a prickly pain in the arse at times, but there was something about her that she couldn't help but like.

Tiptoeing across to Finn's door she paused, listening to see if she could catch any sounds from inside. No. Nothing. Had he just gone to bed then?

But wait - there was something. Very faint, and not coming from his room at all but from downstairs. She cocked her head. It was the distant but unmistakable sound of a typewriter.

Eve hugged herself and did a quiet little dance on the landing. Her plan was working. Right. She should go back to bed.

She paused.

Go back to bed!

It was no use. She knew what she *should* do, but Eve found herself being drawn to the stairs - drawn to that distant sound.

Surely it couldn't hurt to just . . . have a peep? He wouldn't even know she was there.

Before she could think too hard about it, she rustled quietly down the stairs. Eighteen years worth of moving around this house without waking a sleeping child meant she knew exactly where to step to avoid all the creaks and groans.

As she approached her study, the rhythmic clatter of the old typewriter got steadily louder. The door was slightly ajar, and a beam of golden lamplight trickled out across the hallway.

Eve halted a couple of feet away and peered through the gap. There was Finn at her desk, hammering away with a look of blissed-out concentration on his face. She felt her knees go weak with desire at the sight of him.

From the moment she'd met him, something about this man had managed to get right under her skin. Seeing him now - clearly in his element - well, there were no words to describe it.

Seemingly unable to stop herself, Eve took a step forwards, her whole body craving to close the gap between them. Then she winced as the floorboard beneath her gave a creak so loud it almost made her laugh.

Typically, Finn chose that exact moment to pause in his typing for a stretch.

At the noise, his head shot up and he frowned.

'Hello?' he said, sounding uncertain, looking in her direction. Clearly he couldn't quite make out who it was spying at him from beyond the pool of lamplight.

Eve had to fight the instinct to turn on her heel and leg it. Instead, she forced herself to push the door open wider and step into the dimly lit study.

'Hey,' she said.

'Ah crap - Eve!'

'I'm so sorry-'

'Did I wake you-?'

They both spoke over each other.

Eve laughed and shook her head. 'No. You didn't. And I'm sorry to disturb you. I just . . . wondered where you'd gone,' she finished lamely, dropping her eyes to the large stack of typed pages sitting neatly on the desk next to him.

Finn followed her gaze, hastily took hold of the top page and flipped it over so that the words were no longer visible.

'Sorry, sorry,' said Eve, mortified. 'I should go!'

'No! Come here,' said Finn, reaching his hand out to her.

Eve hesitated, then walked over shyly and took hold of his hand. How come this felt *way* more intimate than everything else that had happened between them tonight?

Finn tugged on her hand and pulled her onto his lap, kissing her on the temple as he did so.

'I didn't mean to pry - really,' she whispered.

'Don't worry about it!' said Finn. 'It's just a habit of mine, not showing anyone my work in progress.'

Eve shivered as he trailed kisses down the side of her face and onto her neck.

'How's it going,' she asked, fighting the haze of happiness that seemed to be descending on her brain.

Finn pulled back and smiled at her. 'You're clearly a good influence.' He paused and sighed. 'It's going . . .'

'What?' she prompted. 'You know, maybe I really should leave you to it!'

Finn shook his head. 'No. It's fine. I just - I never talk about this stuff to anyone. Well, other than when Laura forces me to.'

'Yeah. I noticed you're really private about it. I mean - it's fair enough. I'm just nosy. And this is clearly a really important part of your life.'

Finn shook his head. 'Not nosy. Curious and caring maybe?' he said with a smile.

'I'll take that. But this is your thing. I'll go.' She went to stand up again only to land back on his lap with a bump as he wrapped his arms around her.

'Oh no you don't!' he said. 'It's time I got over myself.'

Eve glanced at him and then froze in place. He

looked like he was stealing himself to open up a bit, and she didn't want to stop him. As much as she wanted to give him his space - she was desperate to know more about him and his work.

'Several years ago,' he said slowly, 'before I got my first publishing deal, I was engaged.'

Eve raised her eyebrows but managed to stop all the questions that flooded into her head from escaping.

'My fiancé - my *ex*-fiancé, I should say - thought my work was a bit of a joke. She had this highbrow job working in finance, and she made no secret that she found my work . . . embarrassing.'

Eve's jaw dropped in horror, but before she could say anything, Finn continued.

'So, when I was offered a contract with a big publisher, she insisted I published under a pseudonym.'

'What?!' said Eve, unable to stop herself.

'You're getting the picture why she eventually ended up as an ex,' he muttered, giving her a humourless smile.

Eve nodded.

'Anyway - she didn't want her name connected in any way with my work once we were married. Unfortunately, I was completely wrapped up in her. I would have given her anything to make her happy. I hated that she didn't like what I wrote, so I kept it to myself. I made sure I never let her catch a glimpse of what I was working on. Basically, I split my life in two, and just hoped that if I managed to get some success, she'd eventually be proud of me.'

'And was she?' asked Eve.

'Hell no. The success made things much worse. As it happened, the publisher was more than happy for me to use an androgynous pseudonym. Then - book one went mad. I was offered this huge, life-changing contract for four more books in the same series.'

'Oh my goodness,' said Eve. 'That's amazing.'

'Yeah. Julia didn't think so. She gave me an ultimatum. I could either marry her - *or* I could sign the contract. If I wanted to carry on writing my "embarrassing fluff" we were over.'

'Shit! So . . .'

'So I'm now on embarrassing fluff number five, and Julia is a distant memory,' sighed Finn.

'Good for you,' said Eve.

'I'm not so sure,' said Finn.

Eve felt an icy sensation trickle down her spine. She suddenly needed to put a bit of space between them. Was this thing they'd started some kind of weird, delayed rebound from his bitch of an ex?

Finn watched her with a look of surprise as hopped up off his lap and went to perch in the wooden chair a few feet away from him.

'Eve? Oh god - I didn't mean *her!* Ending that was one of the best decisions of my life!' he said. 'But agreeing to this mad circus the publisher drummed up around me as this "mystery author"? Having to hide who I am from my readers and from the press? It's left me with a few . . .' Finn paused, hunting for the right word.

'Scars?' said Eve gently.

'Issues. Issues around my writing. And that sucks.'

Finn took a deep breath and then looked across at her. 'I did okay to start with. The books were successful. I got on really well with my editor who was my champion. She was always in my corner.'

'Why do I feel a "but" coming?' said Eve.

Finn nodded. 'But. She left just as book four was going through copy-edits.'

Recognition dawned on Eve's face. 'And you were landed with Laura?'

'Got it in one. And she's been full-on from the word go - but it's got a whole lot worse in the last three months.'

'Why?'

'The publisher landed me a film deal.'

'Oh my goodness, Finn?!' Eve squealed. 'That is absolutely amazing.'

'Thanks,' he said, looking like he was at someone's funeral.

'I don't get it - is that not good news?'

'Oh, it is. But it's dependent on me handing over book five,' he paused. 'This book,' he said, laying his hand on top of the stack of newly-typed pages.

'Right . . .?'

'And the minute the deal landed, Laura started

hounding me. There's just something in the way she's behaving, and some of the things she's said . . . well, she reminds me a bit of Julia. I'm not sure she even likes my work.'

'And it all made you freeze up?' said Eve.

'Yep.'

'Well, no great surprises there. Anyone would have a bit of a block after all that!'

Finn ran a finger over the smooth curves of the typewriter in front of him. 'Sorry. I can't believe I just told you all that.'

Eve shook her head. 'Thank you for telling me! You know . . . when you first arrived, I actually thought you were a bit of a book snob,' she laughed.

Finn's head shot up. 'Why on earth would you think that?'

'Your reaction when Lucy dropped our book club read into the studio - FC Chase's most recent one. Your face was a picture.'

Finn opened his mouth, then shut it again. Then opened it . . . and he shook his head.

'Don't try to deny it,' chuckled Eve.

'I'm not,' Finn choked out.

Eve raised her eyebrows at him. 'What? Finn, are you okay?'

He'd gone strangely pale and looked like he was struggling to focus on her. Eve quickly got to her feet, ready to go and grab a glass of water for him, but he reached out and grabbed her arm.

'Finn?'

'Can you keep a secret?' he said urgently.

Eve frowned in confusion but then nodded. 'Of course.'

'I'm serious - this is important.'

She felt a wave of nerves rise in her chest. No matter how he made her feel, she didn't know Finn that well. Not really. What if he told her something awful?

'Depends what it is,' she said, taking in his pale face and the tension that was visible in those silver-blue eyes.

Finn shrugged. 'That was my book. I'm FC Chase.'

CHAPTER 14

*E*ve opened her mouth to say something . . . and then closed it again. This had been going on for a good three minutes solid. So long, in fact, that Finn, who was nervously awaiting her reaction, had gone from nervy - to agitated - to simply concerned.

'Eve? Can I get you a drink or something?' he said, peering worriedly into her face.

Eve shook her head and opened her mouth to say something - then closed it again.

'Oh god,' said Finn running his hands through his hair. 'I shouldn't have told you.'

'No,' croaked Eve at last.

Finn looked like she'd slapped him.

'No - I'm - I'm glad you did! I'm just . . .' she trailed off.

'Just what?' demanded Finn.

'A bit starstruck,' she said awkwardly.

'Oh give over!' he huffed.

Eve shook her head. 'You don't get it. I've been obsessed with FC Chase for years. I mean - I am completely in love with her. And now - she's you. And you're here in my house.' She paused, feeling like she was about to start hyperventilating. 'Oh my god - I just slept with FC Chase!'

'And breathe!' laughed Fin, grabbing a notebook off the desk and fanning her with it.

Eve winced. She felt the blush hit her like a bucket of hot water - not because she'd just slept with her favourite author of all time - but because she'd just managed to tell him, in a roundabout way, that she loved him!

'Sorry,' she muttered. 'Talk about a nice, low-key reaction!'

Finn grinned at her. 'Actually, I quite liked it,' he said, sounding a bit sheepish.

Eve gazed at him, a huge smile spreading across her face.

'Okay - you might have to dial down the adoring looks by tomorrow's session though,' he chuckled.

Eve covered her face with her hands. Man, why couldn't she have played this cool?

'You do promise though, don't you?' he prompted.

'Promise what?' said Eve in a muffled voice, peeping at him between her fingers.

'That you'll keep this to yourself. It would be a disaster if it got out.'

'Are you really that embarrassed by your own work?' she asked sadly, looking at him properly.

'Not even slightly,' he said, 'especially not after hearing you guys talking the other day - I mean, Betsi nearly reduced me to tears!'

'Betsi!' said Eve. 'Did you get her letter - you know, after her husband died?'

Finn shook his head, a frown appearing on his face. 'She was right about all that - the publisher runs my social accounts via a PR firm. But her letter? I guess it just got lost in the giant machine that is their head office. I'm so gutted.'

'She didn't seem to take it personally though,' said Eve, reaching forward to lay a hand on his arm.

Finn shook his head, taking her hand in his. 'I know. But - it would have really meant something to her to get a reply, wouldn't it? Especially with everything she was going through.'

Eve nodded. There was no denying that.

'It makes me wonder how many other readers have tried to reach out to me. They must think I'm such a knob for never answering.'

'Can't you tell her?' said Eve. 'Betsi, I mean?'

'No. Eve - no, you mustn't. Promise me!'

'Of course I won't,' she said looking surprised at his sharp tone. 'But - why the secrecy? You're not with Julia any more, are you? And that's the reason-'

'It's in my contract,' he said, his voice tight. 'A confidentiality clause that basically means my publisher is totally in charge of branding. Which means I'm not allowed to tell anyone. It's even more important now, with the whole film thing lined up. I shouldn't have told you - it's really not fair to put that on you,' he sighed.

'Don't say that. I'm *honoured* you told me,' said Eve. 'But . . . why did you?'

Finn took a shaky breath. 'I want you to know me. Really know me. And this,' he said, leaning forward and placing his free hand gently on top of the stack of typing, 'this is me.'

Eve yawned widely, then out of the corner of her eye saw Finn start yawning too as if he'd caught the tail end of hers and decided to make it a hundred times bigger. She wasn't surprised. After everything that had happened last night, she was completely wiped, but her tiredness was surely nothing compared with his.

After chatting for ages, Finn had finally admitted that he wasn't done with work for the night. So Eve had half-reluctantly, half-gratefully dragged herself back upstairs to bed, leaving him to wind a fresh sheet of paper into the typewriter.

She'd expected to fall asleep the moment her head hit the pillow, but Finn's bombshell was too much to process that easily. She'd eventually drifted into a doze where the characters from his series wound in and out of her dreams, along with everyone from the workshop.

She'd felt him climb into bed beside her just as the sky was getting light outside, and she'd finally fallen into a deep sleep, wrapped in his arms.

Now, as she stared blearily around the studio, she wondered how on earth she was going to manage to stay awake long enough to actually teach today's session. They were all waiting for Horace, Scarlet and Wilf to arrive - and if they didn't turn up soon, she'd be tempted to sneak into the back for a power nap.

Eve had half expected Betsi, Violet and Cressida to be a bit worse for wear after their merry night at the pub, but the three of them had managed to beat her down to breakfast, and Cressida had even started the cooking for her. Now they all sat together at one table, chatting away about book-to-film adaptations while they all waited for the late-comers.

Eve gave a little jump as her mobile started to vibrate in her pocket, and pulling it out she saw Davy's name flashing up. She immediately swiped to answer it and moved away from the others.

'Everything okay?' she asked as soon as she answered.

'Hi mum! So - I hear your new boyfriend has a really cute dog!'

Eve gasped. 'How on earth-?'

'Mum, have you forgotten you live in Little Bamton?'

Eve blew out a breath. 'Spies around every corner,' she muttered.

'That's the one. So, what's his name?

'Finn,' she said, her voice as low as she could make it. She glanced around the room. The three girls looked like they were still deep in gossip-mode, but Finn was watching her, his eyebrows raised.

Eve turned away hurriedly. 'Now's really not a good time. Was there anything else?'

Davy snorted. 'Just - be safe. Use protection!'

'I'm hanging up now!'

Eve swiped at her screen, cringing. She glanced up and caught Finn's eye. Oh god - had he managed to hear all that?!

She started towards him, but right at that moment, Scarlet pushed open the door to the studio and Wilf dashed across the room and flung himself up into Finn's arms.

'Hello mate!' said Finn, burying his face in the dog's soft fur, while Wilf tried to lick his face.

Eve's heart melted, and Finn's warnings about controlling her adoring looks flooded back to her as she watched this little public display of affection. She quickly looked away before anyone spotted quite how gooey she was going.

'He was such a good dog,' said Scarlet as she settled herself down on a stool. 'I think mum and dad are in love with him. My evil plan worked. Mwa ha ha ha,' she deadpanned, rubbing her hands together.

'Planning on getting a dog, are they?' asked Betsi.

'They are now!' said Scarlet with a sly grin.

'Morning Horace!' said Eve, as the last member of their little group ambled in.

'Morning gang!' said Horace sweeping his hat off, and then to Violet's apparent horror, he made his way around behind her stool, bent over and planted a kiss on her cheek.

Finn let out a loud wolf-whistle that made *almost* everyone laugh. Violet however narrowed her eyes and turned around in her seat to glare at him.

'Watch it, young man,' she said.

Eve saw Finn do an exaggerated gulp and had to bite her lip. It was time to start proceedings before this lot got any rowdier.

Her plan for the morning was for everyone to share some of the work from their sketchbooks, and then help each other choose one or two of their studies to develop into a piece to hang in the exhibition.

They were all busy discussing the merits of a gorgeous little pen and ink piece Cressida had done of the double-hump-back bridge when there was a knock at the studio door.

Eve had just broken away from the group to head

over and see who it was when a woman flung open the door and stepped inside.

'Can I help you?' said Eve, her eyebrows raised in surprise.

'Eve Grey?'

'That's me, but I'm teaching a private workshop at the moment,' she said.

'Yes. That's why I'm here,' said the woman, her eyes travelling over everyone's faces as they stared at her. 'I'm here to write about it. For the paper.'

Eve shook her head in confusion. The paper wanted to cover her workshop? But how did they even know about it?

'The local paper?' she asked, feeling a bit blindsided. 'Well, the exhibition opens at 2pm tomorrow. If you'd like to come along then, I'll be happy to share-'

'Are you aware,' the woman cut across her, taking a step further into the room, 'that you have a celebrity in your midst? How does it feel, having an A-lister on your first ever workshop?'

Eve's mouth dropped open. What on earth was happening here?

'I think it would be best if you could come back-' she started.

'Would you believe that the elusive FC Chase is right here in this room?!' the woman interrupted.

At these words, Betsi let out a gasp - which was handy as it went some way to mask the gasp of horror that came from both Finn and Eve.

'That's right,' she continued. 'So. If I could have a word with Finn Casey? Or should I say - FC Chase?'

The room went completely silent for a moment. Eve's mind was racing. She needed to get this woman out of here - but even if she did, it was too little too late. She'd just told everyone Finn's secret.

'Come on, Finn,' said the woman sweetly, her eyes travelling from one face to the next. 'How about an exclusive.'

It suddenly dawned on Eve that she might know Finn was here, but she didn't know what he looked like.

'I'm Finn Casey.'

Eve gasped. Cressida had got to her feet and taken a step forward.

The woman turned to look at Cressida, a look of confusion on her face. 'Oh, but surely-'

'No, I'm Finn Casey.' This time it was Betsi.

A frown appeared on the reporter's face as she glared between the two of them.

Scarlet hopped down off her chair, and Wilf jumped up excitedly to stand next to her. 'I'm Finn Casey - and so is my dog!' she said with a wide grin.

'What on earth-?' said the woman.

'I think it's time you left,' said Horace, also getting to his feet.

'Is it you? Can I have just a moment, Finn - just a few words for your fans?'

'This is private property and a private class. Unless

you'd like me to call the police?' Horace pulled out his iPhone and waggled it at her.

The woman turned on her heel, and throwing a dirty look over her shoulder, she scuttled back outside and they saw her heading back towards the square.

Eve hurried over to the door and turned the key in the lock before turning back to the dumbfounded group. Betsi, Cressida and Scarlet were still on their feet.

Scarlet held out her hand for Cressida to high-five. 'Can't beat a bit of Monty Python,' she said with a grin.

'Thank you.' Finn's voice was shaky and his face was incredibly pale as he looked from Horace to Betsi, then turned to Scarlet and Cressida.

'Was she telling the truth?' asked Violet.

Finn nodded. Eve noticed his eyes had taken on a hunted look. He was clearly trying to work out what he should do next.

'Finn, what-?' Eve flinched as their eyes met and she saw a well of hurt there that felt like a punch in the gut.

'Did you-?' he began, but before he could get the words out, there was a loud banging on the door.

Eve glanced over fearfully but relaxed a tiny bit when she spotted Caro peering at them through the glass. Eve hurried over to let her friend in.

'Lucy just called me!' she said before Eve could even say anything. 'She wanted me to come over and warn you guys. There's a whole bunch of photographers and reporters out in the square!'

'What?!' said Finn, shooting to his feet, the remaining colour draining from his face.

Caro turned to him with a look full of concern. 'Finn, they're all asking for you. They're saying that you're . . . that you're FC Chase?'

CHAPTER 15

Finn ran his hands through his hair, making it stand on end. Then he nodded.

'Yeah. I'm FC Chase. Not much point denying it now, I guess,' he muttered. 'At least, not to you guys.'

The entire room went completely still as every pair of eyes remained glued on him.

'Thanks for trying to help, though,' he shot a weak smile at Cressida, then Betsi and Scarlet.

Cressida shrugged. 'Sorry it didn't help more.'

'Yeah. Well, at least you bought me a bit of time. I'm . . . I'm not sure what to do next. I guess I'd better go and face the music.'

'Wait a minute lad, let's not be hasty,' said Horace. 'I'm sure we can figure this out. Step one - we need to get you out of Little Bamton.'

'But what about all the photographers?' said Violet.

'Just because the idiot who came in here didn't know what Finn actually looked like, doesn't mean the rest of them won't have done their homework!'

'There's another way out of the craft centre,' said Caro. 'There's a fire exit at the back of Sam's unit. It leads to a gate into the churchyard. From there you could scoot around to the car park at the back of the pub and avoid them.'

'Is Sam even in today?' said Eve.

Caro shook her head. 'I think he's still out on site. I've got his keys though.'

'But they're bound to spot Finn when he comes out of the car park,' said Betsi. 'What's he going to do, try to out-run them?'

Horace shook his head. 'My car's parked in there. Finn, take my keys. Borrow the car. Go do what you need to do.' He fiddled in his jacket pocket, drew out a set of keys and tossed them to Finn, who caught them on auto-pilot.

'Oh sure,' drawled Violet. 'And there's no way your Rolls Royce is going to draw *any* attention, is there?'

'Anyone got a better plan?' asked Cressida.

There was silence again.

'Finn. Go with Caro!' she said. 'We'll do our best to distract them.'

'Ooh yay,' said Scarlet, 'fun!'

Finn turned to her. 'Can you look after Wilf for me until I get this sorted out? I need to know he's safe.'

'Of course,' she said with a nod.

Finn bent low over Wilf and the little dog jumped up for a tickle, managing to lick his face in the process.

'Be good, little man!' he said, then straightened up and grabbed his bag. 'When I've figured everything out, I'll call y . . . bollocks, my phone - it's still not working!'

'Take mine!' said Scarlet, quickly handing her mobile over. 'Everyone's numbers are in there!'

'You're a lifesaver!' he said, giving her a quick, one-armed hug.

'Ready?' said Caro.

Finn nodded and then strode past Eve without even looking at her. Eve felt her stomach roll with panic. What the hell . . . ?

Caro peered out of the door. 'Coast's clear. Quick!'

Eve watched as Caro and Finn dashed over to the door of Sam's unit.

'What are you waiting for, girl?' Violet hissed at Eve, making her jump.

'Yeah - go with your man!' said Cressida.

Eve turned to look at them and Scarlet nodded, keeping a tight grip on Wilf's collar as he whined, desperate to chase after his master.

Eve swallowed, trying to digest the fact that the entire group seemed to know that something was going on between her and Finn.

'Seriously, *what* are you waiting for?' demanded Violet.

Eve jumped. 'Horace? You're in charge. Lock this place up for me?'

Horace nodded and gave her a salute as she dashed out after the other two, just in time for Caro to lock the door of Sam's place behind her.

'You're not coming, are you?' demanded Finn, barely meeting her eye.

Eve saw Caro raise her eyebrows, clearly surprised at his tone.

'I'm-' started Eve.

'No time!' said Caro, pointing back outside towards the craft centre entrance - where a large crowd of photographers had just started swarming towards Eve's studio. 'Come on!'

They made their way quickly through Sam's darkened showroom, skirting around the various pieces of hand-crafted furniture and then Caro let them into the workshop at the back. They flew past the various bits of machinery and works-in-progress, heading towards the signposted Fire Exit.

'Is it alarmed?' asked Finn in a worried voice.

Caro shook her head, thumped down on the crossbar and swung the door open.

The three of them piled out onto the little passageway beyond, and Caro slammed the door shut behind them.

'Come on,' she muttered, shepherding the other two along the narrow passageway. 'If we're lucky, the press will all be inside the craft centre by the time you pull out of the car park.'

They reached the old, wrought-iron gate that led into the churchyard, and Eve lifted the stiff latch with some difficulty. The gate clearly hadn't been used in quite some time, and it let out an agonised groan as she pushed it open.

'Shhhh!' said Caro, flapping her hands at the gate.

The three of them dashed along the pathway that followed the churchyard hedge, then Eve held out a hand, indicating for the other two to hang back for a second.

She crouched down behind the huge stone pillar that flanked the main gates that led back out into the square. They needed to cross over the wide path so that they could climb the hedge on the other side. Unfortunately, this meant that they'd be in full view of anyone who happened to be looking in this direction.

She carefully stuck her head around the pillar and breathed a sigh of relief. 'Only a couple left,' she hissed, 'but facing the other way - quick!'

They hurried across the path, not daring to look out into the square as they went.

'Shit, this is much higher than I remember,' muttered Caro, running along the hedge and searching frantically for a place to climb over.

'Over there,' whispered Eve. 'There's a gap just past that hazel tree. Davy and his mates used to use it!'

It was quite a tight squeeze - Eve went first,

followed by Finn, who then turned to give Caro a hand into the lane that led up to the allotments.

'Okay - you two carry on through there,' said Caro, pointing at a stile that led into the next field. 'Follow the hedge down and climb the wooden railings into the pub car park.

'What about you?' said Eve.

'I'm going to wander down here and head into the square. I might be able to keep their attention on me for a couple of minutes and buy you two some time.'

'Eve, go with Caro,' said Finn, his voice firm.

Eve shook her head. 'No chance. I'm coming with you.'

'I don't think that's a good idea.'

Caro gave Eve a sympathetic look, and Eve felt a sudden prickle in her eyes. What the hell? After everything that had happened between them - after everything they'd shared last night - why didn't he want her help?

'Erm, don't you need Eve to let you into the B&B to get your stuff?' said Caro.

Finn huffed. 'Of course, you're right.'

Eve swallowed. Of course, she could just tell him that she'd left the back door to the house unlocked - because . . . well, this was Little Bamton, and she'd always left that door unlocked, just in case Davy ever forgot his key. But she wasn't going to. She needed a few moments alone with him.

'Right. Go. Good luck!' said Caro, ushering them on.

'Thanks for everything,' said Finn.

'No worries,' said Caro, turning and striding back down the lane towards the square. 'Love your books, by the way!' she hissed over her shoulder.

Eve saw a quick smile flicker on Finn's face, but it quickly gave way to confusion before he turned away and climbed the stile into the field.

She hurried after him, and it was a matter of seconds before they were at the back of the pub car park. Other than Horace's Rolls and one or two empty cars, it was completely deserted.

Finn pulled the keys out of his pocket. 'Let's get this over with,' he sighed, hauling himself over the fence.

Eve followed him across the car park at a trot and slid into the immaculate old car the minute he'd unlocked her door for her.

Finn started the engine with a roar and then, after struggling with the unfamiliar gearstick, he crawled towards the exit into the square.

'Ah, shit!' he said as they reached the junction, flinging one hand up in an attempt to hide his face from the cameras that were already trained on them. He yanked the steering wheel in a wild arc and they careened into the square.

It was one thing trying to navigate the sharp, right-hand turn one-handed, but doing so whilst trying to avoid the gaggle of reporters who were streaming out of the craft centre towards them was something else entirely.

'Finn! Watch out!' squealed Eve, leaning over and pulling on the wheel so that they narrowly avoided a cameraman who'd just appeared out of nowhere on their other side.

'Hold on!' grunted Finn, as he changed gears and sped out of the square before the crowd managed to block their escape route.

'Turn left and keep your foot down!' muttered Eve, directing him up the ridiculously steep hill onto the top road that ran past Sam's place. There was no way that even the most determined of the press pack would be able to chase them up there!

Finn whizzed up the hill as Eve turned to look behind them. She'd been right. The two or three photographers who'd tried to follow had fallen back - the nearest one was bent double, clutching his knees.

'We're safe!' she said, turning back to Finn.

'Safe? I wish it was that easy,' he said, keeping his eyes firmly on the road.

'Finn, what-?' Eve began.

'Was it you?' he cut her off, the hurt in his voice sending a shooting pain into her heart. 'Did you tell the press who I am?'

'What?! Of course I didn't,' she said, horrified.

Finn glanced at her. 'So it's just a coincidence - the fact I told you yesterday - after *years* of keeping this quiet - and suddenly a gang of journalists turn up?!' He sounded lost, and scared, and confused, and all Eve wanted to do was reach across and take his hand.

'You *know* I would never-'

'That's the thing, I don't. Not really.'

Eve fought down a sob that was rising in her throat. Now was not the time. If she was going to help him through this, it was time to let her head take over from her heart.

'Turn right here,' she said. 'Down the hill. We're nearly back- we're just approaching from the opposite direction.'

Finn nodded, took the turning and then glanced at her again. 'I'll just grab my stuff and get out of your hair.'

Eve stayed quiet. She wanted to beg him to stay. She wanted to help him sort this out - but how could she when-

'Shit!' she said. 'Stop the car! They're already there.'

'What?' said Finn confused.

'Stop the car!'

He drew to a shuddering halt and turned to look at her.

'A van just pulled into my drive,' she said, pointing down the road.

Sure enough, as they both turned to look, another car followed it.

'Is there any way you can sneak in around the back?' Finn asked her urgently.

Eve nodded.

'Great. You get out. I need to get away before they spot me.'

'But your stuff -?'

'I'll arrange for someone to collect it.'

'But, where are you going to go?' she asked, the quiver creeping back into her voice.

'I'm sorry, Eve, I can't tell you.'

Something felt like it snapped inside her, and Eve hurriedly undid her seatbelt and got out of the car. She was just about to slam the door when she paused. She turned back to look at him. 'It really wasn't me, Finn.'

Finn looked at her, and for a moment his face seemed to soften. 'But I heard you on the phone,' he said doubtfully.

'Phone? What do you -?'

The sound of a car coming around the bend behind them made her jump.

'Finn - GO!' she slammed the door hard, catching a glimpse of his face as it went from confusion to anger to realisation, all in a split-second. He took off with a squeal of tyres.

Two seconds later, the approaching car pulled up next to her.

'Hi love,' said a man, hanging out of the passenger window. 'Any idea where I can find Eve Grey's place.'

'Oh. Erm, sure,' Eve nodded, hoping the look on her face and the fact that she was almost in tears wouldn't give her away. 'I think it's just up there.' She pointed towards her own drive.

'Cheers!' he said as the car started moving again.

Eve waited until she saw them disappear onto her driveway before turning on her heel and heading back in the direction of the village. The idea of facing that lot alone made her feel sick. She needed reinforcements. Even more than that - she needed a hug. She wrapped her arms around herself as her tears finally started to fall.

CHAPTER 16

'They're all out in the garden,' said Jon as Eve stepped, red-eyed, into Violet's kitchen.

'Oh. Okay, thanks.'

She'd been about halfway back when she'd received the text from Horace letting her know that they'd all retreated to Violet's cottage, and Eve had headed straight there. She was just glad not to have to wade through any reporters on her way there.

'Hey, you okay?' asked Jon, a look of concern on his face.

'Yeah. Just . . . one of those days, you know?'

Jon nodded, giving her a sympathetic look. 'I get it. Good news is - they commandeered the teapot and the biscuit tin on their way through - maybe that'll help?'

Eve nodded. She tried to smile back, but all she managed was a kind of weak grimace. 'Is Caro out there too?'

Jon shook his head. 'She nipped in to help Lucy deal with the crowds. Apparently, once you and Finn drove off, half of them descended on the pub.'

'Oh blimey. Poor Lucy!'

'Lucy's a smart cookie,' laughed Jon. 'I guarantee you she'll have made a fortune out of them and not let a single thing slip about you, or Finn, or anything.'

Eve nodded. 'Well - I'd better-'

'Yeah - get back to your group - if there's anything I can do, just let me know, alright?'

'Thanks Jon!'

Eve made her way through Violet's cottage, picking her way around various paint pots and dust sheets as she went.

'Eve!' squealed Scarlet the moment she stepped out through the back door. 'Oh my god, are you okay?' Scarlet rushed to her, Wilf hot on her heels. The moment Eve spotted the little dog, her tears started to fall again.

Eve tried to force a smile as Scarlet hovered in front of her. 'I'm fine. Everything's fine.'

'Rubbish,' said Cressida cooly over the top of her bone china teacup. She was sitting, sunning herself with the others around Violet's large garden table.

'Oi!' hissed Violet.

Betsi got to her feet, walked over to Eve, and wrapped her arms around her like they'd known each other for years.

'Shhh chicken,' she said, stroking Eve's hair as if she was a small child. 'It's all been a bit of a shock, that's all.'

Eve nodded into Betsi's shoulder, wishing she could just stay here, wrapped in this woolly, warm cuddle for the rest of the day.

'So. *Was* it you who outed Finn to the press?' demanded Cressida.

'Of *course* it wasn't, idiot.'

Eve pulled back from Betsi's hug to find Violet glaring at Cressida who, in turn, was staring blandly back at Eve.

'Well - we don't actually know that it wasn't her yet, do we?' said Cressida.

'Didn't you see her face? She didn't have a clue what was going on,' said Violet with a frown.

'Guys,' said Scarlet, looking awkward. 'She's standing right here!'

Eve turned and rested a grateful hand on the girl's shoulder for a second. 'Thanks,' she said, with a weak smile.

'So?' said Cressida.

'No. It wasn't me. And what makes you think I knew anything about all this before the rest of you, anyway?' she demanded.

'Oh come *on!*'

To her great surprise, this came from Betsi. Eve stared at her.

'What? I'm not saying you told anyone anything - but we all knew you and Finn were at it - so he was bound to have told you about the whole mega-star-writer thing, wasn't he?'

'*At it?!*' spluttered Eve.

'You know what she means, young lady,' chuckled Horace.

'But . . . how-'

Horace shrugged. 'This *is* Little Bamton, Eve.'

'Unbelievable,' muttered Eve, slumping down to sit on a step. 'I really do need to look into moving somewhere else.'

'Don't say that,' said Violet, looking horrified.

Eve just shook her head. 'Anyway Cressida,' she said at last, 'why are you so bothered about all this? Quick thinking back there with the whole Monty Python skit, by the way.'

Cressida coloured. 'It's your fault.'

'How many times-' said Eve, starting to get angry again.

'No - not that!' said Cressida quickly. 'I mean, it's your fault for getting me hooked on FC Chase - I mean - Finn's bloody books. I grabbed the first one off your shelf after you'd all been going on about them. I wanted to find out what all the fuss was about, and then I couldn't put the blasted thing down!'

Violet let out a hoot of laughter.

'Is that why you kept disappearing rather than hanging out with us?' said Betsi.

Cressida nodded, shamefaced. 'Yep. Tea time. All night. Lunchtime. I was binge-reading *Indulgence.*'

'But - I don't get it. What's that got to do with you trying to confuse that journalist?' said Eve.

'Because I've already finished book four,' huffed Cressida. 'The last thing I need is for some idiot to upset the author and put him off writing the fifth book.'

'How very selfless of you!' said Violet, shaking her head.

Cressida shrugged. 'I never claimed to be a nice person.'

'You're not fooling anyone,' said Eve.

Cressida turned to her and gave her a rare smile. 'So - what happened after you and Finn made your escape? Did you guys sort everything out? Did he manage to pick up his things?'

Eve shook her head. 'There were more reporters up at my place.'

'Did they see you?' asked Scarlet, looking horrified.

Eve shook her head again. 'I spotted them before we got there, so Finn kicked me out of the car and left without picking his stuff up.' She paused. A lead weight seemed to be settling in her stomach. 'Look, I'm so sorry for all this. It's hardly what you were all expecting when you signed up for the week, is it?'

'Are you kidding me?' said Betsi. 'I haven't had this fun in such a long time.

The others all nodded enthusiastically.

'Yeah - it's not like it's your fault, Eve,' said Scarlet.

'And we're not finished yet,' said Horace. 'We've still got the exhibition to sort out.'

'But you've missed most of today,' said Eve, looking worried.

'We've already talked about that,' said Cressida. 'If you don't mind, we'd really like to carry on working in the studio later this evening - to catch up?'

'Oh. Erm . . . sure. Of course.'

Eve knew it made a lot of sense - not to mention that she owed it to them. But she was already exhausted from everything that had happened - she was functioning on very little sleep, after all. She was dreading having to get her head back into work-mode for the afternoon, let alone carrying on into the evening. Plus, she had hoped to escape for a glass of wine with the girls.

She needed to decompress.

She needed her friends.

She needed to know what she should do about Finn!

'We all think you should take the rest of the day off,' said Horace firmly. 'If you're happy for me to keep hold of the studio keys, I don't mind locking up when we're done. We'd like the challenge of putting the show together as a group.'

'But-'

'You could still tweak it tomorrow morning - before we open to the public,' said Scarlet looking excited.

'You all want to do this?' asked Eve, looking around.

All five of them nodded enthusiastically.

'Okay then. If you're sure. But . . . just don't include any of Finn's work, will you? It wouldn't be fair to him.'

'He'll be back though, won't he?' said Scarlet, looking worriedly down at Wilf, who was flopped in the grass by her feet.

Eve gave her a decidedly wobbly smile. 'Don't worry - there's no way he'd be away from Wilf for too long. But-' Eve took a deep breath, doing her best to stop her lip from trembling. 'But - I don't think he'll be back for any more of the workshop.'

Scarlet looked gutted.

'Where was he planning to go?' asked Betsi.

'He wouldn't tell me,' said Eve.

'But why?' said Scarlet.

'Because he thought she'd outed him, duh,' said Cressida.

'Which we have already more than ascertained she didn't,' barked Violet.

'Right,' said Cressida with a nod. 'But I'm guessing you didn't manage to convince Finn?'

Eve shook her head. 'I've been thinking about it all the way back down here. He said something about overhearing a call I'd made . . . like that's what made him think it was me.'

'Who were you talking to on the phone just before everything kicked off?' said Cressida. 'You were definitely looking a bit shifty!'

Eve snorted in spite of herself. 'That's because my teenage son had just told me to make sure I used protection with my new boyfriend.'

Cressida and Betsi both started to giggle, but Scarlet looked mortified.

'Ah!' said Horace. 'That explains a lot.'

Eve raised her eyebrows at him questioningly.

'I heard you mention Finn's name on the call, that's all. Just thought it was a bit odd as you'd been so busy sneaking around. And you said something about spies.'

'Yeah,' huffed Eve. 'The Little Bamton spy network making sure that Davy knows what his mum's getting up to even though he is all the way over in Greece. Oh god - do you think that's what did it?'

'Could be!' said Horace. 'I mean, you looked all guilty, you mentioned spies, and Finn's name, and then you ended the call in a hurry . . .'

Eve's mouth dropped open as the penny dropped.

'Then it's all my fault,' said Scarlet.

Eve turned to her and was shocked to find her looking so pale.

'I told Davy about you and Finn - and Wilf,' she said, cuddling the little dog, looking like her heart might break.

'It's not your fault at all,' said Betsi, scooting over to sit next to Scarlet, and putting an arm around her.

'No. Not at all,' said Eve. 'The only person to blame for this mess is whoever went to the press about Finn in the first place.'

Scarlet glanced at Eve, looking guilty and unconvinced.

'I'm serious, Scarlet. Though I have to say - it's good to know who Davy's spy is!' she said with a chuckle. 'I didn't even realise you two were friends.'

Scarlet nodded. 'Yeah. It's quite . . . recent.'

'Witterwoo!' said Betsi, earning herself an elbow in the ribs.

'Not like that!' said Scarlet, her face going from white to pink. 'Anyway, at least you can tell Finn what the call was really about when you speak to him - get it all sorted out. Have you heard from him yet?'

Eve shook her head. 'No, and I don't think he's likely to contact me - I was hoping he might have messaged one of you guys, to be honest,' said Eve.

Horace pulled his phone from his pocket and, looking at it, shook his head sadly.

'What about his social media?' said Scarlet. 'Like - is he on Twitter or anything? Maybe he's posted?'

Eve shook her head. 'His publisher does all his posting, apparently.'

'Balls,' said Scarlet, earning her a grin from Violet.

'Erm . . . wrong,' said Horace.

'What?' said Eve.

'He tweeted from his FC Chase account five minutes ago. *"So excited to be staying for a few nights at The Haymarket, Exeter #metime #amwriting"* - and then there's a picture of that big, posh place down by the harbour.'

'Well, at least we know where your car is!' said Violet.

'Well - that's odd,' said Betsi. 'I don't get it. Why'd he do a runner from Little Bamton only to announce where he is to the entire world an hour later?'

Eve frowned. Betsi was right, it didn't make any sense.

Horace's phone buzzed in his hand.

'Huh,' he said, 'Scarlet - I've just had a text from you.'

'It'll be Finn!' she squeaked. 'Quick, read it!'

Horace fiddled with his phone for a second. 'Okay,' he cleared his throat. 'It says -

"Staying at hotel in Exeter for a few nights while I sort everything out. Spoken to publishers and sent them a pic of the place - asked them to tweet it to get the press to leave you guys alone. You shouldn't have to pay for my drama."

'Is that it?' said Betsi, looking a bit disappointed.

Horace nodded, then his phone buzzed again. 'Wait, no -

"Sorry - hit send by accident. Good luck with exhibition. Loved spending time with you guys. Can you send me Scarlet's parents' number so I can call about Wilf and sending her phone back? Thanks for everything. Finn x"

Horace slipped his phone into his pocket and they all stayed silent for a moment. Eve felt like someone had just stomped on her chest. She was glad Finn was okay . . . but the fact that he hadn't contacted her - or even mentioned her - hurt. Like, really hurt.

'Well,' said Cressida, 'at least that should get rid of the assholes from around the craft centre - and hopefully your place too, Eve.'

Eve nodded, not quite trusting herself to say anything.

'There's an easy way to find out. I'll give Lucy a call at the pub to check what's going on over there,' said Horace.

'Good idea,' nodded Eve. 'I'll just have to figure out what to do about the ones at my place later.'

CHAPTER 17

Eve sank onto her sofa and pulled her patchwork blanket up to her chin. It was a desperate attempt to hide from everything that had happened since she'd left the house that morning - but she'd try anything right now! Eve closed her eyes, listening to the creaks and sighs of the old house.

Letting out a huge sigh, she revelled in the moment of peace and quiet. As much as she adored the others for being noisily on her side, it had been a struggle to keep her emotions in check. Saying goodbye and leaving them all at the studio had been quite a relief.

Now, ensconced on her sofa under her tatty old blanket, Eve finally gave in to the tears that had been threatening to fall for hours.

Horace had called the pub to check on the unwelcome visitors, and Caro told him that they'd all disappeared. She'd offered to do a quick lap of the craft centre and report back. When she called him five minutes later, it was with good news - they'd all vanished.

When Horace hung up, he told Eve they'd come up with a plan to check her place was free of intruders too. Sure enough, within twenty minutes, Eve got a call from Sam, Caro's other half. He'd just driven over to check the farmhouse and said that there was no sight of the reporters anywhere in the vicinity. Sure enough, when she'd got back, there were no signs they'd been there other than a stray chocolate wrapper lying on the driveway.

Eve sat up restlessly. It was too hot for blankets and hysterics. She needed to pull herself together.

She grabbed her mobile and quickly fired off a message to the whole book club. Now that she knew she had the evening to herself, the one thing she craved more than anything else was her friends. Within minutes, all five of them had replied, promising to be with her in an hour.

Knowing they'd be here so soon was enough to force Eve to her feet. She had something she needed to do - and it was better she did it before the wine arrived.

Eve headed down the hallway towards her study. A large part of her was absolutely dreading going inside, but Finn would need his stuff sooner rather than later, including the work he'd managed to do while he was here. If he was going to send someone

SUMMER NIGHTS AND PILLOW FIGHTS

to pick it up like he said he would, she wanted to be prepared.

Pushing open the door, Eve bit her lip. The sight of her lovely old typewriter on the desk instantly made her eyes start to prickle. Had it only been last night they'd sat in here together? Last night that he'd told her all his secrets?

Eve swallowed hard and tried to shift herself into practical-mode. She headed for the desk, marvelling at how much the pile of typing had grown since she'd last seen it.

Gently, she gathered the bundle together, resisting the urge to glance at the words. Then she reached for a wide elastic band and wrapped it around the pages. Eve picked up the two plain-black notebooks and placed them on top of the little pile. She'd take these upstairs and pop them into his laptop bag so that they were safe.

Eve glanced around in case there was anything else to pack up, but other than a couple of abandoned, dirty cups and a pencil she was pretty sure he'd borrowed from her own stash, this was it.

Now for the tough bit - it was time to go and pack up Finn's room. Eve turned to leave the study, but as she did so, her eyes caught on a screwed-up ball of paper that was resting against one of the desk legs.

Placing the books and papers back down for a moment, Eve bent to retrieve the piece of rubbish and was about to toss it into the waste-paper basket when she paused. Holding her breath, she slowly unfolded it, her eyes focusing on the typed words.

It started out as a piece of test paper - clearly Finn had been trying out the various keys, probably trying to find a symbol, or how to add a tab or something. But halfway down the page of nonsense, she spotted her own name.

Heart racing, Eve read the few short sentences.

I just told Eve everything. I can't believe I told someone I met less than a week ago. But I want her to know me. The real me. All of me. Anyway, I trust her. There's something about her. I think I'm falling in love. It feels like something is changing, like today is the first day of something new and exciting. Like something is going to happen.

'Well, he definitely got that last bit right!' said Sue, shaking her head as she read over the crumpled page again and then passed it to Caro. 'Something definitely happened - I just don't think it was *quite* the something he'd been expecting.'

The minute the girls had arrived, Eve had thrust the sheet she'd found at them before she changed her mind about showing them - for the hundredth time. Part of her felt like it was a horrible betrayal of his trust - because he'd clearly meant for this page to end up in the bin. On the other hand, the guy had basically accused her of outing him to the press - so she didn't feel *that* bad! Besides, Eve needed their opinion. What should she do next?

'I don't know, Eve,' said Emmy frowning. 'I mean - that's all really romantic and everything, but he leapt to the worst possible conclusion about you - with nothing really backing him up.'

'Other than the fact that he'd told her he was FC Chase less than twelve hours previously - and then overheard one side of that dodgy phone call with Davy,' said Lucy, fairly. 'I mean, I know it wasn't nice, Eve - and I really feel for you - but what a shock for the poor guy! He must have been totally freaking out!'

Eve nodded. 'Yeah. Especially because the fake name isn't a vanity thing - keeping it secret is actually part of his contract with the publisher.'

'Crap!' said Amber. 'Do you reckon he might be in trouble for all this?'

Eve shrugged. 'I'd say it's a possibility.'

'Poor guy!' said Caro.

Eve nodded. Any anger she'd felt towards Finn for thinking it might have been her had pretty much disappeared by this point. All she could think about was what he must be going through, trying to sort it all out. She'd considered calling Scarlet's phone to speak to him - or even just sending a text - but she'd chickened out every time.

'Guys, do you think I should try calling him?' she asked.

'No,' said Lucy bluntly, taking a sip of wine.

'But-' Eve started.

'I wouldn't, love,' Lucy continued. 'Not tonight. Everything's still too fresh. Too raw. He's probably knackered. Goodness knows what he's had to go through with his publisher to sort this out. He's probably angry, and upset, and trying to figure out who might have done this to him.'

'He already knows that,' muttered Eve, slumping back against the sofa cushions, 'or at least he thinks he does,' she added, pointing at herself.

'Nah,' said Sue. 'The guy's smitten. I don't reckon he really believes it was you.'

Eve's spirits lifted a bit at Sue's optimistic take on things.

'I do agree with Luce though,' she said, resting a hand on Lucy's thigh. 'Don't call him. Not tonight. He's got a lot of figuring out to do.'

Eve watched as Lucy turned to Sue and smiled.

'Okay,' said Amber, who was now holding the crumpled typing paper. 'Can we just take a second away from the whole Finn and Eve issue?'

'God, yes please,' laughed Eve, taking another sip of wine.

'Cool,' said Amber, in her usual blunt manner. 'Because as gorgeously romantic as this is,' she said, waving the paper, 'I want to know what's going on here!' She pointed at Sue's hand, which was still resting on Lucy's leg.

The whole room went still, other than Lucy who turned in slow motion to look at Sue, her face glowing.

'Looks like it's time,' said Sue quietly.

Lucy nodded.

'Well . . . we're together,' said Sue as Lucy buried her face in her shoulder.

'I knew it!' squealed both Emmy and Eve at the same time.

Caro gave a whoop of delight and clapped her hands while Amber did her best not to look too pleased with herself.

Lucy peeped at them. 'You all *knew*, didn't you?' she gasped.

The others nodded, grinning back at her.

'Inklings,' laughed Caro. 'Definite inklings. Tell us everything. When did it all start?'

Sue looked at Lucy. 'Christmas?'

Lucy nodded. 'Yeah - I mean, that was when it became a *real* thing, rather than just me pining,' she giggled.

'When I arrived in Little Bamton?' said Caro, her eyes wide now.

'Yep - we fell in love over that mountain of sprouts,' laughed Sue.

'Aw, you guys!' sighed Emmy.

'But . . . why didn't you tell us?' said Amber.

'Because this is Little Bamton!' laughed Lucy.

'Fair point,' said Eve. 'Jungle-drums central!'

'Exactly,' said Sue. 'We didn't want the pressure of

having the entire village in the relationship with us. At least, not while it was all shiny and new. But now . . .'

'Now - well - we're happy,' said Lucy, leaning across to kiss Sue on the cheek.

'I'm so happy for you guys,' said Eve.

'Now we just need to get you sorted out,' said Lucy, nodding at her.

'I'm not sure she needs *that* much sorting out,' said Sue. 'I mean, she *has* just shagged the mega-star-author of our current read. That has to be a book club first!'

Eve shook her head and rolled her eyes.

'Imagine if you guys end up together,' sighed Caro. 'So romantic! Maybe he'll put you in one of his books.'

'I don't know what I was thinking,' said Eve tightly. 'I mean, even if all this drama hadn't happened - I live here and he lives in London. It was never going to be more than a holiday fling, was it?'

'This says otherwise,' said Amber, waving the paper at her.

'Eve, don't miss out on the good things in life just because you're scared,' said Sue, lacing her fingers through Lucy's. 'You can make this work if you want to.'

Eve shook her head. 'Ignoring the fact that *"this"* has already imploded - what with Davy leaving, and trying to start this new business - I just can't turn my life upside down.'

'No offence,' said Amber, 'but I'd say you're life's

pretty much upside down already. Finn might just be your key to getting it the right way up again.'

'Erm,' said Caro, who was staring at her phone, looking alarmed. 'I hate to be the bearer of bad news, but Horace just messaged me. An online gossip site has just posted a piece exposing Finn as FC Chase . . . and there are pictures of the two of you together.'

'What?!' squeaked Eve. 'How?'

'Apparently, there's one of you in the graveyard and another one of you both in Horace's car. Looks like they've been digging into everything - they've even wheeled out his ex for a comment.'

'Asshats!' hissed Amber.

'Poor Finn!' said Eve, thinking about everything he'd told her the previous night about his ex.

'What are you going to do?' said Emmy, staring at her.

Everything she'd just said about keeping her distance and not turning her life upside down fell away in an instant. It was time for her heart to take over proceedings again.

'I'm going to go to him,' said Eve, her voice determined. 'Tomorrow. I'll take him his stuff. He shouldn't have to deal with this on his own.'

'But, what if he won't see you?' said Emmy, her eyes wide.

'I've got a secret weapon,' said Eve. 'I'll take Wilf.'

CHAPTER 18

*E*ve slept like a log in spite of herself. Even as she'd curled up in bed the night before, her mind still racing, there had been something immensely comforting in the knowledge that she had a plan.

Now, as the early-morning sun streamed through the gap in the curtains, she stretched out under the duvet feeling refreshed and relaxed . . . until the memory of everything that had happened yesterday crashed in and knocked the wind out of her. In the light of a new day, the idea of putting her plan into action filled her stomach with a swarm of nervous butterflies. What if Finn didn't want to see her? What if he'd already left Exeter? What if this thing they'd started didn't mean as much to him as it did to her?

She reached out, felt around blindly for her phone without even bothering to lift her head off the pillows, and then peeped at the screen. Part of her was really hoping there would be a message from Finn to say that everything was fine and that he was coming back to Little Bamton. Sadly, that was the same part of her that believed in fairy tales.

Even so, Eve felt a prickle of disappointment when there wasn't a single message. She quickly opened Twitter and navigated to his FC Chase account, but there hadn't been anything new posted since the photograph of the hotel. Of course, this wasn't much of a surprise given that it was his publisher who controlled the account, not him.

Eve knew it was a bit like picking at a scab, but she couldn't resist searching the internet for the post that had gone live yesterday. It wasn't hard to find.

Of course, she'd read it several times the night before, but she couldn't help scrolling down to stare sadly at the photographs of them together. Of all the amazing moments they'd shared this week, these two really weren't the ones she wanted a photograph of. Her, Finn and Caro running across the churchyard path, and her and Finn looking like rabbits in the headlights as they struggled to steer Horace's Rolls through the mass of press in the square.

Just underneath these two photographs was another - this one of Julia, his ex-fiancé. Eve wrinkled her nose in dislike. She was attractive. Beautiful, even. But somehow, Eve just couldn't imagine her paired with Finn. She couldn't believe how vile the woman had been either, trying to make out that Finn had left her after his work took off, rather than because she'd been such an evil cow-bag.

Eve shook her head and tossed her phone away from her. She didn't need to read that rubbish again. Besides, it had absolutely no bearing on the man she'd met - the man she was missing. Even though she'd known him for less than a week, Finn had left a gaping hole behind him.

It was time to get up and face the day. Baby steps. First, she needed to make breakfast for everyone. Then she would pack Finn's things into the car, drive the girls down to the studio and check in on the group's progress from the night before. Hopefully, it wouldn't take too long to give them some pointers to finish things off in time for their grand opening that afternoon.

She still felt incredibly guilty about the next part of the plan, but needs must. She was going to dog-nap Wilf, leave the others to finish up in the studio, and zoom up to Exeter to find Finn. With any luck, she'd be back in time for the opening.

Eve took a deep breath as she pulled on a tee-shirt and quickly bundled her hair back into a bobble. She'd just have to work out exactly what she was going to say to Finn on the way up there in the car. Because, right now, she had nothing. The only thing she could guarantee was that there would be tears if he wouldn't hear her out. Why was adulting so difficult?

Eve trundled down the stairs towards the kitchen,

surprised at just how quiet the house was. Cressida, Violet and Betsi had come home fairly late the night before, and other than a few words to check how she was feeling and to let her know how well it had gone in the studio, they'd all headed straight up to bed.

Maybe they were just having a lie-in. She would get the pastries on, brew them some coffee and take everyone breakfast in bed. She felt like she owed them a treat after everything that had happened.

Eve pushed her way into the kitchen, went to flick the kettle on and then stopped dead in her tracks. There were three bright-pink post-it notes stuck to the side of it.

Already had breakfast - your pastry is in the oven keeping warm. We've all gone to studio for early start. V, C & B

We've borrowed a couple of props from the house. Hope that's okay. Cressida

P.S DON'T come down before 9. We want to get it finished before you see it. V xx

Eve couldn't help but laugh. She was so proud of how enthusiastic this little group was, in spite of all the interruptions. Well, there was nothing for it but to sit back, relax and enjoy her breakfast in peace. Eve snorted even as the thought drifted through her mind.

'Who're you kidding?' she muttered to herself, knowing full-well that she wasn't going to be able to sit still until she was back in the car and on the road to Exeter.

Eve marched towards the entrance of the craft centre. She was excited to see what they'd put together, but she couldn't help but admit that her heart wasn't quite as in it as it should be. She was distracted. Nervous. Impatient to get this whole thing over and done with.

But no. Eve paused underneath the willow arch and gave herself a little shake. These guys deserved her full attention. No matter what happened with Finn, this, right here, was important.

She strode towards the studio and then stopped in surprise. They'd completely papered over the front windows so that there was no way to see what was going on inside. Eve let out a little laugh. Well, that was one way to make sure they weren't bothered by any more unwelcome visitors.

She glanced at her watch. Five past nine - surely they'd be ready for her by now? Just in case they weren't, Eve knocked on the door and waited. The sounds of excited scuffling made her grin.

The door cracked open, and Scarlet's eye appeared.

'Oh - it's you!'

'Nice to see you too!' laughed Eve.

She saw Scarlet grin apologetically through the gap. 'Give us two secs.'

Much to Eve's amusement, Scarlet shut the door again. She tried to swallow down her impatience - and this time it had nothing to do with wanting to rush off and put her plan in action - now she was genuinely intrigued to see what was behind that door.

'Okay,' said Scarlet, pushing the door open for her. 'We're ready.'

'Sure?' said Eve.

Scarlet paused, peeped back over her shoulder as if to be certain, and then turned back to Eve and nodded, leading her into the studio.

Eve followed her inside but then stopped, staring around her with her mouth wide open.

It was . . . stunning. And unique. And unexpected. The two main side walls showed off a mixed collage of the whole group's work. It wasn't the free-for-all mash-up she'd half expected. One wall was completely monotone. It ran from the lightest pencil sketches and white chalks at one end, through darker pen and ink work, and on to heavy charcoal studies against dark, moody backgrounds at the other.

The other wall was arranged in a similar manner, but this was where all the colour lived, running in a gradient through all the colours of the rainbow - a rainbow that showed the beauty of Little Bamton in the summertime.

'What do you think?' asked Cressida, a note of uncertainty in her usually confident voice.

'I . . .' started Eve, struggling to find the words. 'It's . . .' she turned to the group gathered near the covered windows. 'Stunning.'

There was a collective sigh of relief as everyone seemed to let go of the breath they'd been holding.

'Seriously,' she said, 'I'm so proud of you guys.' Eve took a step towards the back wall and shook her head. This was something else entirely.

In front of her was a patchwork of pieces from their very first session. They'd been taped together into one huge sheet.

'We weren't sure about including those to begin with,' said Betsi, coming up to stand next to her, 'but you said this should be about process.'

Eve nodded. Her eyes travelled across the scrawled experiments, the buckled pieces of paper where they'd used too much water and the harsh lines where a pencil had almost pierced the background. She loved it - but there was one thing about it that made her incredibly sad. This was a wall that told the story of their little group - but, of course, someone was missing. She knew it was stupid to feel like this because it had been her who'd told them to leave Finn's work out of the exhibition - but he was so conspicuous in his absence that it hurt.

'Anyway . . .' said Horace, sounding unsure.

Eve knew she should say something, but she was really struggling to hold it together.

'It's great.' She had to force the words out.

Wilf wiggled his way over to her and nudged his nose against her leg as if he knew something was wrong.

Eve let out a small laugh - which could just as easily have been a sob - and bent down to tickle his ears.

Wilf's tail went into overdrive as he licked her hand, then he turned and ran off into the little storage space at the back of the studio, squeezing through the partially closed door, only to turn around and hare straight back to her again.

'What on earth . . .?' she laughed, relieved to hear her words come out a little more naturally this time.

'Oh,' said Scarlet. 'I've got some dog biscuits in my bag . . . I expect that's what he's after.'

'Figures,' said Eve.

'And - back to the studio,' said Horace.

'Yeah,' said Cressida, stepping forward. 'Like Betsi said, we weren't sure about this back wall, so we put together an alternative, and we thought you could choose between them for us.'

'Oh. Okay-' said Eve, looking around.

'Can you close your eyes for a minute while we sort the other one out?' said Scarlet.

'Erm-'

'We just want you to get the full impact,' said Violet.

'Of course,' said Eve with a sigh, resigning herself to the experiment.

'Take a pew,' said Horace, bring one of the high stools over for her to perch on.

Eve hopped up and dutifully closed her eyes, listening to the rustling of paper and screeching of a piece of furniture being dragged across the floor.

'Okay,' said Betsi a few minutes later. 'Open them.'

Eve opened her eyes and did a double-take.

'How-?'

The wall in front of her had been transformed. The experimental daubs had gone, only to be replaced by dozens of little sketches and drawings, interspersed between pages that looked like they had been typed on a typewriter.

In front of the wall, standing on a low table, was her old typewriter itself, a crumpled piece of paper wound into the rollers.

CHAPTER 19

'I don't understand,' said Eve. She didn't know where to start. How *could* they have used something this personal? She quickly removed the paper from the typewriter. Sure enough, it was the crumpled few sentences she'd discovered the previous day - where Finn had typed out how he felt about her.

Eve held it tightly, her hand shaking. She'd left it on her desk the previous night, lying next to the typewriter like some kind of talisman. And they'd *taken* it?!

She couldn't bring herself to turn to face them. She needed to get her anger and hurt under control first. Taking a step forward, she stared at the work on display. Every piece was an attempt to capture her and Finn in some way. One of Violet's caricatures showed them toppling into the river. A sketch that looked like it might have been done by Horace attempted to capture the moment she'd leant over Finn's shoulder and guided his hand. A large piece in pastel showed their names linked together, the E and F curling around each other like vines.

'I . . .' Eve swallowed. This was agony. It was the beautiful story of their few days together. She cleared her throat. 'I thought I asked you not to include any of Finn's work,' she said in a low voice, staring at the watercolour of a flower in a sunlit field. The one she and Finn had painted together.

Her eyes moved to rest briefly on one of the typed pages. It looked to be a copy of the online post outing Finn as FC Chase.

Wilf nosed her leg, and she tore her eyes away from the wall and bent down to cuddle the little dog, desperately seeking some comfort. She needed to get back outside for some air before she lost her temper. Before she said something she'd regret.

'We'll go with the first version,' she choked out. 'You don't have Finn's permission-'

'Actually, they do.'

At the sound of his voice, Wilf yanked himself out of Eve's embrace and hurtled off towards his master.

Eve peered around, only to find Finn staring at her from the open door to the storage space.

'Finn?' she said. 'When . . . how? You're here?!'

Finn nodded at her, a huge smile on his face.

Eve turned to the rest of the group, only to find them scuttling through the front door. Cressida, who was bringing up the rear, winked at Eve over her shoulder.

'Finn?' she said, turning back to him.

'I'm so, so sorry Eve,' he said, not moving.

Eve quickly shook her head.

'No,' he continued. 'I really am. Everything was so sudden and so messed up . . . I didn't know what was going on and . . . I don't know,' he paused and ran his hand through his hair. 'I was freaking out . . . that's not an excuse, I should never have accused you, but that phone call-'

'It was Davy!' said Eve quickly.

Finn nodded. 'Yeah. I know. Scarlet told me.'

'Is that why you came back?' she asked.

Finn shook his head again. 'No. I'd already come back to Little Bamton when she told me. The minute I drove away from you, I wanted to turn back - but I had to get the situation under control first. I had to speak to my publisher and explain what was happening.'

'What did they say?' asked Eve, wide-eyed.

'They already knew.'

'What?!' said Eve, slumping back down onto her stool.

Finn nodded and took a tentative step towards her.

'They'd been trying to contact me, but of course, my phone was out of action, and you'd stolen my laptop,' he smirked.

'Oh no!' said Eve, trying to take it all in. 'So Laura had been trying to warn you all that time?'

Finn shook his head. 'Not Laura. More like her boss's boss's boss.'

'But-?'

'I know who outed me,' said Finn.

'You do?!' said Eve, her eyes wide, struggling to keep up.

Finn nodded. He stepped towards her and held out his hand for hers. Eve hesitated a moment before taking it and allowing him to lead her off her perch and back towards the wall. With his free hand, Finn tapped one of the typed pages hanging there.

It looked to be a copy of an email. Eve's eyes scanned the lines that spelled out the link between Finn Casey and FC Chase. When she reached the name at the bottom, she gasped.

'No way!' she turned to Finn.

'Yes way, apparently,' he said, lacing his fingers more firmly through hers. 'It was Laura.'

'But . . . why?!' said Eve. 'And how did they even know.'

'The *how* is easy. They were monitoring her emails. It seems that there have been quite a few complaints from other authors about her conduct! As for why - well, apparently she thought it would be "good for my career." When they questioned her about it, she said she had taken matters into her own hands because I was being so slow with the fifth book!'

For a second, Eve didn't know what to say and

stared back in disbelief at the email. 'Are you in trouble with the publisher?' she asked.

'Are you kidding me?' laughed Finn. 'They're falling over themselves to do anything they can to keep me sweet. That confidentiality clause worked both ways. Obviously - Laura's already been booted.'

Eve nodded. 'Of course. But what are they going to do about the whole FC Chase thing now that the whole world knows it's you?'

'Well,' he said, squeezing her hand and looking a bit nervous all of a sudden, 'that all depends.'

'On what,' said Eve.

'On whether you'd consider publicly dating *Finn Casey Writing as FC Chase*?'

He laughed as he said it, but Eve could see the shadow of fear on his face.

She turned to him fully and, taking his other hand in hers, pulled him close and looked up into his eyes.

'I don't want you to pretend to be anyone other than exactly who you are,' she said, cringing as her voice wobbled a bit. She cleared her throat. 'Because I'm addicted to that person.'

Finn reached out and touched his index finger to her cheek. Eve shivered as the tiny, warm contact sent a tingling sensation through her.

'Paint,' he said with a smile, then gently grazed her lips with his.

. . .

'Cheers guys!' said Amber, holding her pint up to the little group who sat, red-faced and triumphant, in the pub garden. 'Awesome show - congratulations!'

'Hear hear,' said Caro, navigating her way towards them with a laden tray in her hands. 'These are on the house.'

Eve took her glass of wine with a grateful smile and snuggled into Finn as he wrapped an arm around her.

After Finn's shocking revelations about Laura, the rest of the group had crept back into the studio just in time to catch Finn kissing Eve.

When the excited cheering had died down, a very red-faced Eve had been treated to the full story of everything that had happened the previous evening. As soon as Finn had finished talking to his publishers, he'd left them to deal with the fall-out and called Horace. Then he'd hopped back into the Rolls and hot-footed it back to Little Bamton.

All Finn had wanted to do was make things right with Eve, but the minute he arrived, the others had convinced him to wait a little longer - and together, they'd concocted the grand plan.

'That was possibly the most romantic thing I've seen in my life, you know,' sighed Emmy, bringing Eve's attention back to the pub's sunlit garden.

'You should have seen it before we had to remove the really personal bits,' said Scarlet, feeding Wilf a crisp. 'We had to take down the email, the post about Finn, and the love note,' she sighed.

Eve laughed. 'Only because I wouldn't give it back!'

'Thank god!' said Finn, pulling a mock horrified face. 'What would my fans have said?!'

'That it was the most romantic thing you'd ever written,' sighed Betsi.

Finn grinned at her and raised his pint. 'Thank you.'

'Anyway, I think you all did a wonderful job filling the gaps with your early pieces,' said Eve. 'Joining the two ideas was the perfect solution.'

'I still can't believe you agreed to us leaving the rest of it up, Finn,' said Cressida, 'not with the press turning up - and that lovely lady from your publisher.'

'Yeah, who was she by the way?' asked Caro.

'Helen? That's my new editor!'

'Ooh, fancy!'

'She's amazing. She was the one I was hoping to get when my old editor left . . . before I got lumped with Laura!'

'So what's the plan now, Finn?' asked Horace. 'Back to London?'

Finn shook his head. 'I've got a book to finish before I start on my very first series as Finn Casey! So, I've asked around and apparently, there's this fantastic local B&B where the owner will steal your mobile phone and laptop whenever you get stuck!'

Eve snorted and dug him in the ribs.

'So you and Wilf will be staying?' said Scarlet excitedly. 'How long for?'

Finn glanced at Eve and she smiled softly back at him.

'What do you reckon?' he asked.

'Until we figure out where this story is headed next.'

THE END

ALSO BY BETH RAIN

Little Bamton Series:

Little Bamton: The Complete Series Collection: Books 1 - 5

Individual titles:

Christmas Lights and Snowball Fights (Little Bamton Book 1)

Spring Flowers and April Showers (Little Bamton Book 2)

Summer Nights and Pillow Fights (Little Bamton Book 3)

Autumn Cuddles and Muddy Puddles (Little Bamton Book 4)

Christmas Flings and Wedding Rings (Little Bamton Book 5)

Upper Bamton Series:

A New Arrival in Upper Bamton (Upper Bamton Book 1)

Rainy Days in Upper Bamton (Upper Bamton Book 2)

Hidden Treasures in Upper Bamton (Upper Bamton Book 3)

Time Flies By in Upper Bamton (Upper Bamton Book 4)

Standalone Books:

Christmas on Crumcarey

Seabury Series:

Welcome to Seabury (Seabury Book 1)

Trouble in Seabury (Seabury Book 2)

Christmas in Seabury (Seabury Book 3)

Sandwiches in Seabury (Seabury Book 4)

Secrets in Seabury (Seabury Book 5)

Surprises in Seabury (Seabury Book 6)

Dreams and Ice Creams in Seabury (Seabury Book 7)

Mistakes and Heartbreaks in Seabury (Seabury Book 8)

Laughter and Happy Ever After in Seabury (Seabury Book 9)

Seabury Series Collections:

Kate's Story: Books 1 - 3

Hattie's Story: Books 4 - 6

Writing as Bea Fox:

What's a Girl To Do? The Complete Series

Individual titles:

The Holiday: What's a Girl To Do? (Book 1)

The Wedding: What's a Girl To Do? (Book 2)

The Lookalike: What's a Girl To Do? (Book 3)

The Reunion: What's a Girl To Do? (Book 4)

At Christmas: What's a Girl To Do? (Book 5)

ABOUT THE AUTHOR

Beth Rain has always wanted to be a writer and has been penning adventures for characters ever since she learned to stare into the middle-distance and daydream.

She currently lives in the (sometimes) sunny South West, and it is a dream come true to spend her days hanging out with Bob – her trusty laptop – scoffing crisps and chocolate while dreaming up swoony love stories for all her imaginary friends.

Beth's writing will always deliver on the happy-ever-afters, so if you need cosy… you're in safe hands!

Visit www.bethrain.com for all the bookish goodness and keep up with all Beth's news by joining her monthly newsletter!

facebook.com/BethRainBooks
twitter.com/bethrainauthor
instagram.com/bethrainauthor

Printed in Great Britain
by Amazon